TILL DEATH DO US PART

WILLIAM MALMBORG

DARKER DREAMS MEDIA

Copyright © 2023 by William Malmborg

All rights reserved.

No part of this book may be reproduced in any form or by any electronic or mechanical means, including information storage and retrieval systems, without written permission from the author, except for the use of brief quotations in a book review.

Publishers Note: This is a work of fiction. Names, characters, places, and incidents either are the product of the author's imagination or are used fictitiously. Any resemblance to actual persons, living or dead, events, or locales is entirely coincidental.

ISBN: 978-1-7348763-3-8

TILL DEATH DO US PART

ONE

1

"MOMMY!"

Beth opened her eyes upon a world that was being upended, the cry from her daughter just one element of the madness that was unfolding as pictures fell from the walls, books and knickknacks from the shelves, and a glass from the side table, the untouched inch of amber liquid splashing out upon the floor as it shattered.

"Mommy!"

2

"I DIDN'T EVEN KNOW you could get earthquakes in St. Louis," Jill said.

"Most don't," Beth replied, phone in one hand, cigarette in the other. "They not only happen, but this area had one like two hundred years ago that was the biggest quake to ever hit the US."

"What? No way!"

"No joke. It's because of the New Madrid Fault. And if another big one like that one hits, this place is going to be toast."

"Seriously?"

"Yep. Mostly because everything around here is brick and was built without earthquakes in mind. And with this little six pointer today, it could be a sign that the big one is going to hit at any moment."

"Well ... if it didn't happen in 2020, then it's probably not going to happen at all."

Beth let out a chuckle.

"Though if it does, fingers crossed it happens while Don is there and something crushes his head like a melon."

Beth didn't reply.

"And then, after that, you can travel the world with me while living off the interest from everything you inherit."

"You know I hate to travel."

"That's because you only ever travel with Don. With me, you'd get to see a *whole new world*."

Beth cringed at her friend's singing voice, one that would have probably taken a viral walk of shame if she hadn't — thankfully — allowed herself to be talked out of auditioning for *American Idol* several years earlier.

A voice only a mother could love, Beth thought to herself.

Sadness followed.

"So, earthquake aside, how are you doing?"

"I'm okay I guess."

"Have you seen your mother yet?"

"No. We got in too late last night."

"I still can't believe you Uber'd all the way down there."

"Didn't have much choice."

"I'd have driven you."

"Yeah, but this way Don had to pay for it."

"Oh ... well then ... *you go girl.*"

Beth smiled.

"So," Jill asked, "any more info on what exactly happened?"

"No. Just that they found her in the hallway by the attic stairs." She sighed and stretched, her back aching from sleeping on the sofa. "Hopefully, I'll know more later this morning."

"Keep me posted."

"Will do."

3

"YOU CAN'T JUST USE my card like that!" Don shouted at the phone on his desk, his anger getting the better of him.

"Your card?" Beth asked, voice echoing up from the speaker. "Last I checked, both our names were on it."

"Yeah, well, not for long," Don said.

"What, you're going to take me off of it now?"

"You bet your ass I am."

"Go ahead," Beth said. "That will look great for me once I tell everyone that you not only refused to drive me down to see my mother, but then cut me off from our accounts as well, all while I have our daughter to feed and take care of."

Don didn't reply to that.

"And by the way, I know that the only reason you refused to come down here was because you were going to see your little fuck-buddy lawyer skank that your mommy hooked you up with."

"Beth," he said. "You know she and I are just colleagues. Have been for years."

"Jill saw you two together!"

"She's also my lawyer."

"While I was in jail!"

Don sighed. "We're not going to do this again."

"Is she there right now? I bet she is. Probably sucking your cock beneath your desk while we're talking. Just wait until the jury hears about this."

Another sigh. "Beth. There is no jury. And the judge will never let you get custody of Belle. No way, no how. The sooner you realize this, the sooner we can put this ugliness behind us."

"You're not getting custody of her!" Beth shouted and hung up the phone.

Don stared at his phone for a few seconds and then turned toward Kelly, who had come into his office during the call.

"Beth says hi," he said.

"Somehow I doubt that," she said, letting out a small chuckle.

Don added his own.

"So, what was that all about?"

Don told her about Beth's mother and how Beth had taken an Uber from Chicago to St. Louis on his dime.

"You really should have gone down there with her," Kelly said once he was finished.

"I know, but ... " his voice faded.

"But what?" she asked.

"Nothing," he said, waving things away. "So, what's up?"

"Your mother called me. Said she thinks you and I should have a meeting about your case. Even made us a reservation at that fancy Italian place she takes all the important clients to."

"Olive Garden?" Don asked.

"Ha!"

"Want me to nip this in the butt?" he asked.

"It's bud, not butt, and no way. If this is a meeting about your case that means we can charge it to the firm and I for one will never say no to a free five hundred dollar plate of pasta. Reservation is at eight."

4

"MOMMY, is grandma's house going to fall down?" Belle asked, while dipping a chicken nugget into a small square of honey.

"No, no, not at all," Beth said.

"Are you sure?"

"Positive."

Belle considered this for several seconds, all while systematically dipping and then eating her chicken nuggets.

"Houses fall down during earthquakes," Belle noted.

"I know, but not grandma's house," Beth said, eyes looking down at her cheeseburger, her trembling hands making no move toward picking it up.

"Was it an earthquake that made grandma fall down?"

"No, that was just an accident."

An accident while on the stairs to the attic with a giant bag of kitty litter in her arms, which was a puzzling detail that she still couldn't figure out.

Did you have cats while growing up? the doctor asked earlier, once Beth had finally been able to visit her mother in the ICU.

We did, Beth had confirmed. *Two of them.*

The doctor considered this for several seconds and then said, *Right now the focus has been on the injuries sustained to her body in the fall, but once we get beyond that you'll probably want to start looking into the possibility of dementia having started to set in.*

The word dementia had knocked everything from her mind and forced her into a chair.

Now, at the McDonald's near the hospital, she tried to process it, especially the possibility that her mother had been living alone with dementia for an unspecified amount of time, body wandering around the big house, mind never fully aware of when or where she was, which eventually led her to trying to bring a giant bag of kitty litter up into the attic.

But why the attic?

No litter boxes had ever been up there back when they had had cats, the cats themselves forbidden to go into the attic given the mess of books, board games, old kid stuff, various holiday boxes, old paintings, and stored furniture that created maze-like corridors with what seemed like hundreds of hiding spots, the few times one of the little furry fiends managed to slip by the stairway door always resulting in hours of searching, the well-fed beast unwilling to be lured back out with the promise of food or treats.

Then again, one couldn't really say what was going through the mind of someone with dementia. The stairs themselves might not really have been anything more than stairs that needed to be climbed, the destination beyond playing no part in the thinking process.

And the kitty litter might not even have been kitty litter in her mother's mind, but simply something she grabbed that needed to be stored in the attic.

Though how had she gotten the kitty litter?

Had it been a new bag that had been purchased from somewhere, or had it been an old one that had been sitting unused for years after the cats had died?

So many questions, each one leading down a path of more questions.

Bills.

Had she been keeping up with them?

The house itself was paid off, had been for about fifteen years, but what about the taxes? What if the IRS suddenly swooped in and took everything?

Were there protections in place for someone who had started down the dementia path, or would the cold bastards simply say that a family member should have known what was going on and taken action?

They're not wrong.

Guilt arrived.

Years earlier, the journey from Chicago to St. Louis would not have been much of an ordeal given that it was a straight shot down I-55, but with her driver's license having been revoked following her accident, and Don's refusal to spend his off hours driving to and from the Gateway City, the time between her last visit and now had been over two years.

Over three years, actually.

And as if that wasn't bad enough, the previous visit might have been the last one where her mother would have known who she was; a visit where she had gotten drunk to the point of telling her mother off for driving her father away before vomiting all over herself.

"Mommy, I need more honey."

Beth blinked and looked down at Belle's lunch spread, one which was a jumbled mess of chicken nuggets, cooling fries, and empty plastic honey trays.

All this while her own cheeseburger continued to go uneaten.

"Mommy."

"Okay, hold your horses," Beth said, and pushed herself up from the plastic seat to go get more honey packets.

Not long after that, she was tossing her uneaten cheeseburger into the trash along with the empty wrappers and packets from Belle's meal, a short walk back to the hospital before them.

5

"MOM, NO!" Don said, struggling to keep his voice calm. "Please! Kelly says that taking her off the card would look really bad and might actually give her some leverage in getting custody."

"If you don't call the bank and take her off the card, then I will not only call the bank myself, I will shut down all your accounts."

"You can't do that."

"I can and I will."

"But she won't have any way to pay for anything while she's down there!" he snapped.

"Exactly. You can't have her running around like that racking up debt that you know she can't pay."

"But her mother is in the hospital and she has Belle with her."

"Whisked her away and crossed state lines right in the middle of a custody battle. If Kelly was half the lawyer she claims to be, she would have had protections in place against such action."

Don knew this was exactly what his mother had wanted Beth to do, only her hope had been that Beth would drive herself even though her driver's license had been revoked, and that they could then use that as further evidence against Beth in the custody battle. Instead, Beth had beaten her at her own game, which would have been pretty amusing if it wasn't now causing this particular mess and making it so his own access to funds might be in jeopardy.

I shouldn't have said anything.

I should have just driven Beth down there after the call.

Instead, he had told his secretary that he was going to need her to reschedule all his meetings and court appearances for the next several days, which led to her calling his mother, which had led to his mother calling him and refusing to allow him to take the time off, which had led to him firing his secretary, which his secretary had brushed off with a statement about how his mother was her employer not him, which had put an end to things since she was right.

"By the way," his mother said, "you still haven't told me which school you are going to select for Belle."

Don wanted to ask what the point of his getting full custody of Belle was if they were just going to send her off to a boarding school, but decided losing one argument today was enough and simply said, "I'm still going over the suggestions."

"Need I remind you that the clock is ticking on admissions? These places aren't ones you can simply decide to enroll in at the last minute."

"I know."

"If you don't pick one by next Friday, I'll be choosing one for her myself."

Don let out a sigh that was completely audible across the phone lines and said, "I'll let you know."

6

BETH STARED at the amber liquid in the glass, lips wanting to sip it, needing to sip it, yet somehow resisting.

Why she was doing this to herself she did not know, her initial thoughts when first spotting all the various bottles in her mother's liquor cabinet being to dump them down the drain. Instead, she tested herself, pouring a glass after Belle went to bed and keeping it near until she went to bed herself.

Only to wake up to the earthquake while on the couch — a couch she was going to sleep on again that night even though it would wreak havoc upon her back.

She just couldn't sleep in her mother's bed.

Nope.

And since Belle had her old bed in her old bedroom, she was stuck with the couch.

It wasn't so bad, though.

Sure, it killed her back, but she had it all to herself, which was a nice change of pace ... until it led to thoughts about Don sharing their bed with Kelly.

Not that she really cared about him having sex with others, since she had no desires whatsoever when it came to being with her husband. Instead, it was the audacity of their actions and the fact that even with him flaunting his infidelity to the world; he was still kicking her ass in the divorce.

All because of her numerous DUIs and the *reckless homicide* conviction that had put her in jail. Don could literally be getting a sloppy blowjob by the lawyer skank while in court and no one would care. It was crazy.

Making things worse, the lawyer that Jill had helped her get had made it pretty clear to her that she could not win. And by win, she simply meant get custody of Belle. That was all Beth cared about. Without Belle, her life would be meaningless. An empty void that she would fill with booze until it ended her.

Of this, she had no doubt.

But with Belle in her life ...

She stared at the amber liquid; her desires to take a sip kept at bay.

. . .

7

"YOUR MOTHER actually tried hooking me up with a case involving a cat," Kelly said, following Don's brief mention of how his mother-in-law had apparently fallen down the stairs while lugging a giant bag of kitty litter up them.

"Tried?" he asked.

"Yeah, but I wouldn't touch it. No way, no how."

"You said no to my mother?"

"Yep."

"Why?"

"The client is trying to get custody of a cat simply so she can have it destroyed."

"Are you serious?"

"Yep. All because her soon-to-be-ex husband loves it."

"How do you know she wants it simply so she can have it destroyed?"

"Because she has a history of this. Early in the marriage, which isn't saying much since it hasn't even lasted a year, she let it outside several times even though it's an indoor cat in hopes of it disappearing while her husband was at work, but then since it kept coming back, she took it to the pound one day claiming it was a stray. And not just any pound. She went out of her way to find a kill shelter. Luckily, the cat was chipped, which she apparently didn't know was a thing, so they contacted her husband after scanning it."

"Jesus."

"Yeah."

"I can't believe you told her no," he said.

Kelly shrugged. "It wasn't the first time, and it probably won't be the last."

"Seriously?"

"Yep. She knows I'm the best and that if I don't want a case, I'm not taking the case."

"Does that mean you actually wanted mine?"

"Everyone wanted yours."

"What? Really?"

"An easy win while working a case as a personal favor to your mother ... fuck yeah."

Don looked around, a bit startled by how loud her 'fuck yeah' had been. No one seemed to have noticed. "Still think it's an easy win?" he asked.

"Totally. Working this is like being on vacation. I mean, sure, Beth's continued stubbornness in the face of guaranteed defeat is annoying and this new stuff with her mother could prove a bit troublesome - sympathy wise - but in the end, the outcome will still be the same. You will have full custody of your daughter once this is over."

Don nodded.

"That is what you want, isn't it?" Kelly asked.

"What? Oh yeah. Of course."

Kelly eyed him for a moment.

"Beth is not fit to be a mother," he added.

Kelly continued to eye him, and for a moment he thought she was going to question this, but then their food arrived, shifting their focus.

8

"SO, IS SHE GOING TO LIVE?" Kelly asked

later once their food was finished and their plates cleared.

"Who?" he asked.

"Beth's mother."

"Oh. Not sure. I haven't really gotten all that much from Beth on the situation beyond that she fell down the stairs."

"Hmm."

"Is it important?" he asked.

"I just like having all the details when working a case." She paused. "But don't you worry about it. I'll have Liz find out everything there is to know."

"Poor Liz. Do you ever let her go home, or is she chained to her desk?"

"Chained to her desk, but that's okay, because she totally digs the kinky stuff."

"Ha!" He then noticed the look in her eye and asked, "Seriously?"

Kelly grinned.

"Liz? Really?"

Kelly nodded.

"Wow. I never would have guessed that."

"I wouldn't have either, but then one day something slipped out while she was in my office, which led to us having a little discussion."

"What? She like call you Mistress or something by accident?"

"No, something literally slipped out, as in plopped down right onto the floor with a heavy rubber thunk."

"Huh?"

"Never mind," she said, waving a hand. "Anyway, don't worry about Liz. She's so good at research and uncovering stuff that she'll learn everything there is to know in like ten minutes."

A chime echoed.

Kelly frowned while looking down at her phone.

"What?"

"Your mother."

"Seriously?"

"Yeah. She wants me to call her."

"Why?"

"No idea."

9

"MOMMY!"

Beth jolted awake, body falling from the sofa, her mind thinking 'not again' and 'the BIG ONE' at the same time.

Only it wasn't.

Nothing was shaking.

The house was still.

"Mommy!" Belle shrieked again.

Beth sprang up from the floor and headed to her old bedroom, concern present given the cries, any relief at the fact that the house wasn't falling down around them gone.

"What is it?" she asked upon seeing Beth in the hallway, her face white as a sheet as she peered through the open bedroom door, her arms cradling Kat, which was a stuffed animal that was supposed to be a cat but looked more like a teddy bear with a really long tail.

Belle simply pointed, her finger directing Beth's eyes toward the wall that the bed was pressed up against, an old painting that Beth's long-gone father had done for her when she was a kid still hanging on the wall, Beth having stubbornly protested her mother's desires of having it put up in the attic after her father abandoned them.

"Belle, there's nothing there," she said.

"It was trying to get me through the wall," Belle said, fear present within the words.

"Oh, honey, you were probably just dreaming."

"No. It was clawing through."

Tears arrived.

"I want my daddy," she pleaded.

Beth bristled at that. "Daddy isn't here right now." Then, "Come on, let's get you back in bed."

Belle protested, her feet refusing to make the necessary steps toward the bed, the fear unlike anything Beth had ever seen from her daughter before.

And then she heard it too.

It was an odd clicking noise, one that certainly was coming from the wall behind the bed.

Unlike her daughter, however, she realized right away what it was given the wind gusts that had proceeded the sound.

"Honey, that's just some branches scraping against the house outside. Hear that? It's windy out there and everything is overgrown."

Belle didn't buy it.

What nine-year-old would when the threat of monsters was still a very plausible possibility within their own mental world, one that they knew parents wouldn't believe given how often such things unfolded in the TV shows and movies they watched.

Beth had been the same way as a kid, only her monster was the Blob, the heating ducts throughout the house posing as entry points for the flesh-eating jelly-like space alien.

Click, click, click.

Belle whimpered, her grip on Kat growing tighter.

Beth gave a mental shake of the head, her mind knowing there would be no coaxing Belle back into bed after all this. Instead, she would let her join her in the family room, the small loveseat across from the sofa the perfect size for a frightened nine-year-old.

And come tomorrow she would find a saw in the old woodshed, and cut down whatever overgrown piece of vegetation it was that had sprang up alongside the house during these last several years, thereby removing any future monster threats from waking Belle up as the two continued their stay in her old childhood home.

TWO

1

"NOTHING?" Beth questioned.

"Not yet," the doctor confirmed, "but this is not uncommon with head injuries. It will probably take a few days before she wakes up. In the meantime, she is stable and has been since the day she was brought in, which is a very good sign, so while she's not out of the woods yet, every hour that passes without issue means she is getting better and better to the point where we will be able to wake her up."

"When?" Beth pressed.

"We just can't say."

Beth didn't like that answer. Hated it in fact. But knew there wasn't much she could do about it.

"Any suggestions?" Beth asked, fearing the silence might signal an end to their discussion, which she didn't want given how difficult it was to lock down a face-to-face with the busy doctor.

"Regarding?" he asked.

"What I should do next?"

"For starters, don't hang around the hospital."

She blinked.

"You'll just drive yourself nuts if you do. Get out, enjoy the sights of the city, visit the Arch, do stuff around the house, hike some river trails ... do whatever it is you need to do to take your mind off what is going on here, because it is a situation that you can do absolutely nothing about and sitting around waiting for news will take a toll on you. And your daughter."

"But ..." another blink.

"Trust me. Enjoy things now while you can because once your mother wakes up and goes home, there will be quite a bit of work for you and your family. Going into all that already drained will just make it that much more difficult."

Beth nodded, the doctor's words making sense.

At the same time, it felt wrong to be leaving the hospital; to be leaving her mother alone in the ICU.

Only she isn't really alone.

Far from it.

The layout of this ICU was one of the best she had ever seen, one that made it so an attendant was never more than a few feet away should there be any type of emergency, and even when nothing was going on, her mother was frequently being attended to by various staff members. Not the doctor so much who simply would look at the charts, his feet barely taking him into the small, machine-cluttered room, but the other ICU staff members were constantly going in and out to visit and take care of various things.

All while she and Belle were stuck in the small waiting room, the allotted time for visits short given that it was the ICU and thus not an actual hospital room where one could stay with a loved one up until the visiting hours were over.

The doctor was right.

Staying at the hospital was a fruitless endeavor, one that would simply drive her mad, especially while having to keep Belle occupied at all times.

But then what?

She would simply replace sitting around the waiting room with sitting around her mother's house, one that was filled with nothing but memories that she didn't care to be reminded of.

And booze.

Lots of booze.

Lots of work too, though; work that would help occupy her mind.

Starting with that stupid weed tree that had gone crazy alongside the house. After that, the yard itself would probably need to be cut at some point, which she could knock out, the task one that would be good for clearing the mind.

Unless that was already being tended to ...

Had her mother been capable of cutting the grass during the last several months or did she have someone come to do it?

Guilt at the fact that she didn't know the answer to this arrived, the unknown state of her mother's mental and physical abilities prior to her fall down the attic steps something that should not be her reality. No child should ever have a lack of knowledge about something like this, at least not one that claimed to love and care about their mother.

Find out, she told herself.

Her mother obviously didn't live in a vacuum.

If she had, no one would have called the police

after finding her sprawled out upon the second floor landing.

Nope.

Her body would have stayed there waiting for the smell to get so bad that a neighbor called the police to find out what was going on.

Unless the kitty litter absorbed the smell, that Arm and Hammer stuff being quite strong, the scent of it still present within the hallway three days after being scooped up.

Beth shook that grisly thought away, her mind startled by its ability to effortlessly conjure up such a horrible scenario.

At the same time, it did bring up the odd situation of the kitty litter and her mother's attempt at getting it up the stairs.

Was it truly dementia that had caused such a thing? And if so, what other random things had she been spending money on? Or not spending money on?

She needed to find out about all her bills.

After chopping down the weed tree and cutting the grass.

2

CHOPPING down the weed tree was a bit more of a chore than Beth had anticipated, the trunk far thicker than the average weed tree, and the old saw she found far duller than required for a quick, clean cut.

She didn't give up though, and after about twenty minutes of mindless back-and-forth motions with the saw, the tree came down, a sense of accomplishment dominating her mind for several minutes.

And then it faded.

In its place, she pictured the amber liquid in the bottle, one that could be easily poured into a glass.

No.

No.

No.

She grabbed the downed tree in preparation of dragging it to the tangled brush area behind the house, a sudden realization that Belle was no longer in the corner of the yard that she had seemingly been anchored to for the last half hour catching her off guard.

"Belle?" she called.

Nothing.

"Belle!" she called again, voice much louder this time as she rounded the house and scanned the entire backyard.

"Over here," Belle called.

Beth followed the voice, rounding the next corner of the house, startled to see Belle talking to an older man who was standing near the fence.

"Belle, come here right now," Beth said, voice stern.

"Mommy, this is Mr. Flynn," Belle said. "He's grandma's friend."

"I see," Beth said, her sweaty palm taking hold of Belle's tiny hand, grip firmer than it needed to be, almost to the point where it would cause her daughter discomfort.

"Ah, Beth," Mr. Flynn said. "So nice to see you again after all these years."

Beth didn't reply.

"You don't remember me, do you?" Mr. Flynn said, an amused grin on his face.

Beth studied the man for several seconds, mind waiting to see if anything triggered a memory. Nothing did.

"You and your friends used to steal apples from my tree down on the corner while waiting for the bus," he said, fingers air-quoting the word steal. "Though why you would ever want to sink your teeth into those bitter hunks of gnarled fruit, I could never understand."

Beth nodded, memories returning.

The apples hadn't been eaten, but tucked into backpacks and used for battles outside the school during lunch, and then, once that became dull, thrown at cars during gym anytime they were forced to run the cross-country mile around the school fields.

She had shattered the passenger side window of a pickup truck once, the man behind the wheel actually skidding the car to a halt in the field and giving chase, his finger pointing her out to the gym instructor who had gotten between the man and the group of girls, all of whom had backed up Beth and helped put the blame on an annoying goody two-shoes girl who must have eventually shucked off the good girl persona given her eventual rise to fame within the porn industry.

A beeping echoed.

Mr. Flynn glanced down at his watch and thumbed off the alarm. "Anyway. I just came by to see if there was any word on your mother. My grandson is the one that found her after cutting the grass the other day and we have been worried."

That answers one question, Beth noted to herself. Then, "She's stable, but still in a coma. A chemical one, they say, to let the body do its healing thing."

"I see," he said. "We are all rooting for her."

"Thank you."

We?

She wondered who else was in her mother's circle.

"And if you need anything, just let me know." He handed over a slip of paper that had a phone number on it. "Meals, a friendly ear, babysitting" - he nodded toward Belle - "anything at all, just ask."

"Thank you," she repeated, pocketing the slip of paper. "I do have a question."

"Oh?"

"You might not know the answer, but my mom fell while bringing a giant bag of kitty litter up into the attic. Do you have any idea why she would have been buying kitty litter? I've looked all over the place, but it doesn't seem like she has a new cat."

"Hmm, that is a bit puzzling." He put a finger to his lips. "Let me ask my grandson. He helped her out with all her shopping."

"Okay, thanks."

"In fact, I'll ask him to swing by. That way, you can ask questions directly."

"Perfect."

Beth watched the man take a few steps toward the sidewalk and then, once he was out of earshot, turned around and scolded Belle for talking to a complete stranger.

"But he's grandma's friend," Belle protested.

"I don't care who they say they are. If it isn't me or daddy, you never talk to them while alone."

"What if it's daddy's friend? She's nice."

Beth bristled a bit. "No, just me or daddy."

Belle pondered this.

"Do you understand?" Beth pressed.

Belle nodded.

Beth studied her for a moment, questions on if she truly did dominating her mind.

"Mommy?" Belle asked.

"Yeah?"

"I'm hungry."

3

BETH HAD STARTED to drift on the sofa, the weed tree task earlier in the day coupled with the disrupted sleep of the last two nights and the stress of everything overall catching up with her when the doorbell rang.

Startled, she sat up, her mind momentarily forgetting where she was, but then everything quickly cleared when she heard Belle opening the front door and greeting whoever it was that had come to call.

Furious, Beth raced down from the family room to the hallway, nearly tripping over the runner, body making a spectacle of itself as it came in view of the entryway and the doorway, a tall, yet very awkward and adolescent-looking young man standing there.

"Mrs. Crane?" the young man asked.

"No," Beth said. That would be her mother. She advised of what her name was and then asked who he was.

"Mitch," the young man said. "My grandpa said

you wanted to see me. I cut Mrs. Crane's grass and helped her with shopping and things."

"Oh, yes." She shook away her momentary confusion. "Come in, come in."

He did, seemingly weary. "Um ... I usually cut the grass on Fridays if you will still want me to do that."

"I think I can manage the grass," she said, but then, seeing the look on his face, backtracked a bit and added, "Actually, you know what, let's keep things the way they are since I probably won't be here that long and the grass will still need to be cut once my mom's back home."

His face brightened.

Will she actually be back?

If she has dementia, she obviously won't be able to stay here alone.

It would be a retirement home for her.

A place that could handle dementia patients.

"How much was my mom paying you?" Beth asked, shifting her focus back onto the current situation.

"Twenty-five," Mitch said.

"A week?" Beth questioned, startled. She had gotten ten dollars herself for doing it when she was a teen.

Then again, that was over twenty years ago.

"Um ... yeah," Mitch said, suddenly uneasy. "That includes edging the sidewalk and driveway and things."

It better! she said to herself. "Okay, that seems fair."

He nodded, the uneasy look still present. "I will come by on Friday then ..."

"Wait, I wanted to ask you something."

"Oh?" Concern appeared.

"Did my mom have you pick up kitty litter for her?"

His face went pale. "I didn't know she was going to try to carry it herself. I would have helped if I had known."

Beth held up a hand. "It's okay. It's not your fault." *How did you think she was going to move it around?* "I'm just curious. Was this the only time she had you buy it or was it like a regular thing?"

"No, just this once."

"Did she say why?"

"No, not really. Just asked if I could run to the pet store and get some bags of litter. The stuff with Arm and Hammer in it. She made a point of that several times."

"I see."

He waited, clearly uneasy.

"How many bags?"

"Um ... she wanted five."

"Five?"

"Yeah, but she only gave me enough money for three."

"What about food?"

"Nope. She just wanted the litter."

She pondered that, trying to make sense of it.

"If I had known she wanted it up in the attic ..." he started, voice fading without finishing.

"It's not your fault."

It's not your fault ...

How many times had she heard that while growing up after her father had left?

It didn't matter how true it was, the mind always had a way of making one feel guilt no matter what because deep down inside, one always knew that things could have been different. One little statement, one little question, one little action ... could equal a different outcome.

No amount of assurances would change that.

"So ... um ... " Mitch voiced, hands fumbling about.

"That's all I guess," Beth said. "Thanks for bearing with my questions."

"No problem. Friday then?"

"Yep."

Nothing else was said, Mitch heading back to wherever he lived while Beth once again started pondering the oddity that was the kitty litter.

Dementia.

It had to be.

She had reverted back to when they had cats.

But then why not ask him to buy food?

And why bring it up to the attic?

4

"MOMMY!"

No! No! Not again!

Belle was halfway down the hallway this time, face pale, Kat clutched, body trembling.

"Mommy," she whimpered. "It's still there, and it's going to get me."

"No, honey," Beth moaned, blinking several times, a yawn threatening to cut off her words. "It's just your imagination."

Belle shook her head.

"Come on, let's go see."

Another shake of the head.

"No?" Beth questioned.

A third shake of the head.

"How about I go look first and then you can come after me?"

No reaction this time beyond the frightened stare.

"Okay then, here I go." Beth slowly walked the rest of the way down the hallway and then entered her old bedroom, memories of her childhood wanting to flood into her mind, yet somehow held at bay.

Standing in the middle of the room, she waited and listened.

"See honey, there is nothing in — "

Click! Click! Click!

Beth froze, eyes staring at the wall.

Nothing followed for several seconds, and then another round of clicking echoed.

Had she cut down the wrong weed tree?

Was there even any wind out there?

Moving carefully, she went to the window on the left side of the bed and opened it.

After that, she waited.

And waited.

And waited.

Some wind sprang up, and with it, the clicking sound echoed once again.

Wrong tree?

She couldn't believe it.

How could she —

Her thoughts stopped as she poked her head out the window and looked at the outside wall, an area that was shadowed yet still visible enough in the nighttime sky for her to see that there was no weed tree scraping up against the house. She had cut the right one down.

She stepped into the middle of the room, staring at the wall, a slight jump within herself arriving each time the clicking noise reached her ears.

An animal?

One that had made a nest in the wall?

No.

The clicking seemed too dependent on the wind outside for it to be an animal, unless it was an animal nest, a piece of it being disturbed by the wind and clicking against the wall.

If so, she needed to not only get rid of the nest — one that hopefully would have been long since abandoned — but also figure out how an animal would have gotten inside the walls, and block it off.

This meant a trip up onto the roof at some point.

Did her mom even have a ladder?

If not, maybe Mitch would have one that she could borrow.

Or better yet, she could have him go up there and look around.

And if he falls?

Better him than me.

A brief chuckled followed, one which she quickly scolded herself for.

She would be the one going up there.

"Mommy?"

She jumped, body spinning around to face her daughter.

"I want to go home," Belle said.

"I know honey, but we can't until grandma is better," Beth said.

"I want daddy."

5

BETH DECIDED against slipping out onto the roof via the window once she was in the attic, the steepness of the roof when she poked her head out sending a chill down her spine.

Concern for her younger self followed, her mind amazed that she hadn't plunged to her death - or worse, ended up in a wheelchair - while smoking as a teen.

Nope.

She closed the window, and twisted back around, feet ready to take her back to the stairway.

Kitty litter.

Bags of it were stacked up along the wall to her left, in an area that one could barely stand in due to how low the roofline was when connecting to the outer wall of the house. Dozens of bags. Way more than Mitch had bought if his statements on the totals were true.

Dust was thick upon all but two of them, two that her mother had managed to get up the stairs before the third and final one caused her to fall.

But why so much?

And why had it been up here for so long?

THREE

I

"MAYBE SHE PUT it up there to save just in case she ever decided to get another cat after Bishop died," Mr. Flynn said.

"Hmm, maybe," Beth replied, doubt present.

"She was pretty devastated," he added.

"Really?" Beth asked.

"Oh yeah," he said, nodding. "After you left home, Bishop was everything to her, and she everything to him." He paused a moment. "They were inseparable, especially after Spooky died. He was always by her side and when he got so old that he couldn't jump onto things anymore, she had me build him a cat ramp up onto the sofa and another for the bed so that he could easily join her on each."

Beth had had no idea.

Bishop and Spooky had been given to Beth the day that her father had left, the two kittens an attempt by her mother to keep her mind occupied following the abandonment. It had worked.

Beth still remembered the excitement that had

hit the moment she walked through the front door after school that day and saw the various cat perches and toys that had been brought into the house, and then heard the squeaking of the kittens from behind the kitchen door, her mother having her walk quietly into the room, the two kittens weary of her at first as she sat down on the linoleum floor, but then eventually coming up to her and falling asleep in the folds of her skirt.

"I remember helping her bring in all those perches," Mr. Flynn said.

"You helped my mom bring them all in?" Beth questioned, somewhat startled by the revelation that he had been in the house on the day that her father had left them; in the house following a night of arguing that had been so loud, Beth had had tears running down her cheeks as she sat on the edge of her bed, hands covering her ears yet failing to block out the intensity of what she was hearing.

"I did," he confirmed. "I saw her struggling with them as she came home from the pet store and offered to help."

"And then again when she donated them to the shelter after Bishop died?"

He nodded.

"I wonder why she didn't donate all the extra kitty litter?"

"Huh," he said, seemingly caught off guard by that. "Good question. I never really thought about that before."

"Another one of those weird mysteries, I guess," Beth said while waving a hand, her thoughts on pressing Mr. Flynn to see if there had been more between him and her mother quickly dismissed since it didn't really matter. Not anymore.

Not ever really.

If her mother and Mr. Flynn had had a thing going, that was their business. And honestly, after her father had left them, her mother had been free to do as she pleased.

Was Mr. Flynn the actual reason her father had left?

That question wasn't as easy to dismiss, though once again, she told herself it didn't really matter.

Not anymore.

Not ever.

"Anyway," Mr. Flynn said, "that's my theory on why the litter is up there."

Beth nodded.

"Any word on how she's doing?" he asked, changing the subject. "She able to talk yet?"

"No."

"Well, please keep me posted."

"Of course."

Beth headed back home after that, eyes glancing at the apple tree, mind trying to recall a fun moment from when they were 'stealing' apples, but instead focusing on the time when she was stung by a wasp while reaching for one of the apples.

Tears had erupted, and she had run home only to be rebuffed by her mother who scoffed at her for crying over something so trivial and made her go back to the bus stop, her drying tears noticeable as she climbed up the steps, which naturally resulted in teasing that lasted for weeks.

Why hadn't she been allowed to stay home?

Had her mother been waiting for her to leave so Mr. Flynn could stroll on over while her father was at work?

Beth shook her head, trying to rid herself of the thoughts, the imagery of the two of them together not something she really needed or wanted to dwell upon.

Yet dwell she did, her mind determined to horrify her with its own visualizations of the activities that might have been taking place within the house while she was at school.

Making things worse, she knew a surefire way of stopping the imagery, but did not want to go that route.

One glass.

No.

It was never just one glass.

Or two.

Or three.

It was all of it.

Always all of it.

Once that first sip touched her lips ...

2

A CALL CAME in from the hospital that afternoon. Her mother was starting to regain consciousness, her body fighting against the chemical coma they had her in.

Beth was there twenty minutes later.

"She's in and out, and doesn't make a whole lot of sense when speaking just yet, but she is aware given her eye movements and struggles to communicate," the doctor said.

Beth nodded, her lungs heaving from the full-on sprint she had made once she entered the hospital, several people having actually demanded she slow down.

She hadn't.

More words from the doctor followed, mostly statements of caution on how it would be some time still before they knew the extent of any damage that had been caused by the fall, and what her cognitive state was leading up to it.

Beth nodded through all of this, silently wishing he would hurry it along so that she could go see her mother, while at the same time knowing this was important stuff.

In the end, the visit was anti-climatic, her mother sleeping most of the time that Beth sat next to her, the brief moments when she did open her eyes yielding nothing but looks of confusion as she glanced Beth's way.

3

"SHE DIDN'T SAY anything at all to you?" Mr. Flynn questioned, popping a pill into his mouth following a round of beeping from his watch.

"No, nothing," Beth said, disappointment present.

"Well, even so, this is a big step in the right direction."

"I hope so."

Not much else followed, Beth thanking Mr. Flynn for watching Belle at the last minute while she had gone to the hospital, Mr. Flynn letting her know it had been his pleasure and that he would be happy to do it anytime. He also told her that his grandson could be used as a driver for anything she needed so that she didn't have to keep spending a fortune on Uber rides.

4

"MOMMY, why does the monster live up in the attic?" Belle asked.

"What?" Beth asked, caught off guard by the question.

"The monster in the wall behind my bed."

"Honey, there is no monster. Now eat your egg roll."

"I don't like it."

"You love egg rolls.

"This one tastes funny."

Beth actually had to agree. The egg rolls they had gotten from the place near the house had a very different flavor than the ones they typically got from Cafe Jasmine back at home. They weren't bad, but they also weren't very good.

"Then eat more of the chicken," Beth suggested, the chicken being sweet and sour, though Belle simply ate the pieces plain as if they were chicken nuggets.

Belle popped one into her mouth and started chewing.

Beth did the same, only hers was covered in sauce.

"Is the monster really scared of me?" Belle asked.

"What?"

"Mr. Flynn says the monster is scared of me.

That's why it stays in the walls and lives up in the attic."

"Mr. Flynn said that?"

"Yep. After he went up and talked to the monster."

"What? Up into the attic?"

"Yep." She tried the egg roll again and grimaced.

"Mr. Flynn went up into the attic?" she asked, just to be certain.

Belle nodded. "After I told him about the monster and how it scratches on the wall."

Beth wasn't sure why, but she didn't like that he had been up there. Nothing that was up there should make her feel this way, yet even so, it felt off. Almost like a violation.

Then again, he had gone up there to try to ease Belle's fears about the 'monster' in the walls, which was sweet of him to do, even if it did completely contradict Beth's attempts at trying to convince Belle that there was no monster.

The question was, had it worked?

Would Belle be fine sleeping in the bed that night, or would she once again wake Beth up in the middle of the night with her cries of terror?

FOUR

I

"I'M MAD AT THE MONSTER," Belle said the next morning as Beth struggled to get ready for another visit to the hospital.

"Mad?" Beth asked. "Why?"

"He woke me up again last night, even after I asked him not to. I even said please." She spooned at her cereal, seemingly uninterested in the meal after a few bites.

"Well, monsters can be like that," Beth said. "Now hurry up and finish your cereal."

"I don't like it."

"Honey Nut Cheerios is your favorite."

"The milk is gross."

"That's because you're used to whole milk."

"I want pop tarts."

"There are no pop tarts."

"Can we do McDonald's?"

"Honey, no. Eat your cereal."

Belle made a face.

"Belle," Beth said, adding a layer of sternness to the word.

Belle looked like she was going to protest some more, but then started spooning the cereal into her mouth, several exaggerated grimaces being made.

Beth sighed and then took a sip of her coffee, her own grimace arriving. The egg rolls and the milk weren't the only things that tasted off down here; the coffee she had been making every morning was terrible. She didn't know if it was the beans, the water, the half & half, or the Mr. Coffee pot itself, every cup just seemed wrong.

A familiar ringtone echoed.

Jill.

"Hey, what's up?" she asked.

"What's up is that I think your soon to be ex and that little lawyer skank that he's fucking are trying to get me fired," Jill said, voice loud enough to be heard in the kitchen.

"Whoa, whoa, hold up," Beth said while leaving the kitchen. "Okay, it's just us now."

"Just us?"

"We were having breakfast and your voice echoed a bit."

"Oh Jesus, sorry about that. It's just that I'm royally pissed off right now." She sighed. "Shit, let me start over. How is your mother doing? Your last text said she's finally woken up?"

"She's stable. Nothing beyond that though. Isn't really talking at all yet, and when we say she has woken up, it really just means she opens her eyes from time to time, looks around and makes some sounds and gestures every now and then before falling back asleep."

"Still a very positive development."

Beth couldn't really muster the same enthusiasm about the situation, but voiced agreement. She then asked, "So, tell me what happened?"

2

"IT WAS YOUR MOTHER'S DOING," Kelly said. "She apparently had one of her social media wiz kids get onto Jill's friends list with a sock puppet account a few weeks back, which opened the door for several statuses, comments, and photos she has set to friends only and wouldn't want made public - especially to the airline she works for." Kelly paused, taking a bite of a hot dog, the two having stopped off at a popular stand near the courthouse where they both had upcoming appearances. "She also apparently has had them searching all the various dating and hookup sites to see if she is on any of those. Never know what one might find within those areas, especially if nudity and sex photos are allowed."

"Jesus," Don said, shaking his head. "We have sock puppet accounts on dating sites?"

"Yep. Easiest way to win a case. Find the husband on one of these sites, start talking to him, have him meet up to fuck an escort we have on retainer in a room that has a camera in it, and boom, our client gets everything she asked for and more."

"You do this?"

"Me? No. Never. But others in the firm do. And if it ever looks like I'm going to lose a case, your mother would insist I use such tactics, which would not go well. Just the fact that she did this behind my back has me royally pissed off."

"I can see that," he said.

"I mean, going after her friend like that. It's totally uncalled for."

"I agree."

She eyed him for a moment before taking another bite of her hot dog, almost as if studying him to see if this was true.

"What was it that they posted today?" he asked after his own bite. Beth hadn't elaborated while screaming at him earlier.

"So you know how Jill's a pilot," Kelly said after chewing and swallowing her bite.

"Yeah."

"Well, they found a photo of her, a female copilot and two female flight attendants that she had meme'd with: *The cockpit is now a box office.*"

"Okay?"

"Box office," Kelly said with a chuckle.

"I don't get it."

"A box office," Kelly said.

Don just stared at her, confused.

"Never mind."

Don finished his hot dog and then asked, "So they sent that to the airline?"

"No. They simply posted the screenshot of her profile with the photo on various social media sites while tagging the airline. That way it's all in public and the airline has to respond rather than sweeping it under the rug. That's the way you do it these days if you want to cause problems for a specific employee. No emails to corporate or management or whatever. Simply tag them and the company on social media. Poor service at a restaurant, tag the restaurant; poor attitude from a customer service rep on the phone, tag the business; no smile from a cashier at the grocery store, tag the grocery store. You don't even really have to have evidence of whatever happened, just hinting at it on social media will cause the company to totally freak."

"Wow, I never would have thought of that." Then, after a few seconds, "Did she get fired?"

"I have no idea. I just found out about it this morning. Though given that you are now getting angry calls from Beth about it, it clearly caused some problems for Jill, so — "

A jingle echoed, cutting her off.

Kelly looked at her phone for a moment and then said, "Fuck."

"What is it?" Don asked.

"It's Liz. She says my client just arrived for today's hearing sporting pink hair while wearing a tight t-shirt that clearly shows off the outlines of some new piercings."

"Oh, shit."

"Yeah." She tossed the last of her hot dog into the trash. "I gotta go."

"Good luck," he said as Kelly hurried back into the courthouse, his mind momentarily marveling over how she managed such speed while wearing a pair of heels that most would barely be able to stand in, let alone sprint in.

And then his own phone rang.

Beth.

He sighed and sent it to voicemail, and then put the phone on silent as he headed back into the courthouse himself, his steps unhurried given that he still had about thirty minutes before he had to be in the courtroom, his case today one where he was representing a child molester in a lawsuit against the city and the family of his latest victim now that the city's criminal case had been thrown out on a technicality.

Don was sickened by his client and the fact that he had to represent him in this endeavor, but the man's family was well to do and travelled in the same social circles as his mother, which is why he now had the nauseating job of not only winning the pervert a settlement but helping smear the victim he had taken advantage of.

3

DON WAS SENDING her calls straight to voicemail and while Beth knew it was likely because he was in court, it still pissed her off, which was why she decided to go on a voicemail rampage with the sole purpose of filling up his inbox so that anyone else who called wouldn't be able to leave a message.

Sometimes she wouldn't even talk since words were not necessary in such recordings and would simply leave the phone connected to the voicemail until the time ran out on that particular recording.

Eighteen calls.

That's how many it took before she got a message that his inbox was full.

Satisfied, though also feeling a bit childish, she headed into the ICU to visit her mother; the attendant letting her know that she was doing very well and that her eyes seemed to be more focused on tracking what was going on.

"She isn't speaking yet?" Beth asked.

"Not yet."

"Does she understand if someone says something to her?"

"We can't say yes to that at the moment, though it is possible."

Beth nodded.

A few seconds later, she was sitting in a chair next to her mother who stared at her, Beth trying to figure out if her mother knew who she was or was simply staring out of concern for her predicament and confusion as to what was going on.

To try to help with this confusion, Beth said, "Hi Mom, you're doing really well and will be out of here soon."

A twitch of the eyes was the only reply to this, one that Beth could not ascribe anything of significance upon.

4

"THROWING UP?" Beth asked a few hours later, a call from Mr. Flynn having jolted her awake as she dozed in a waiting room chair, her brief retreat from the ICU while they bathed her mother having turned into a fitful nap.

"Yes," Mr. Flynn confirmed. "She's been a good girl though and made it to the toilet each time."

That was something, at least. "I'm on my way back right now," she said, standing.

"No, no, stay with your mother. Belle is in good hands and I think the worse of it has passed. Just wanted to let you know."

"Are you sure?" Beth asked, easing back into the chair.

"I insist." Then, "Here, she wants to say hi."

Beth waited a second and then yanked the phone from her ear as Belle announced her presence with a booming voice.

"Honey, we don't need to shout when on the phone," Beth said a second later.

"Sorry," Belle said. "I threw up today."

"I heard. Are you feeling better now?"

"Yep. Mr. Flynn gave me lots of 7-Up, which tastes the same as the 7-Up at home, and now we are playing Clue."

"Clue?" Beth asked. "We didn't bring that with us, did we?"

"It was up in the attic. And it's wayyy different from the one at home."

"Is it now?" Beth asked.

"Mommy, can we do pizza for dinner?" Belle asked, changing topics.

"I'm not sure if pizza is a good thing to be eating when you're sick."

"But I feel so much better and my tummy is super empty."

"I bet it is," Beth said, rolling her eyes. "Let me think about it, okay?"

"Okay!"

"How's your mother doing?" Mr. Flynn asked once he was back on the phone.

"About the same," Beth said, suddenly exhausted despite the unexpected nap she had taken in the chair. "She opens her eyes and looks around from time to time, but that's it."

"Well, a step in the right direction, it sounds like."

"Yep."

Not much else was said, the call eventually coming to an end.

Beth stood, ready to head back to check on her mother, but then paused, a realization that Mr. Flynn had been up in the attic again.

Why?

Was it because he had seen the games up there the other day and headed up to grab one when needing something to occupy their time, or was the game just a result of him having gone up there for another reason all together?

But what reason could that be?

Nothing popped into her mind, yet the question did not fade. Something was up with Mr. Flynn. She didn't know what, but she felt it. Something that had to do with her mother and the attic.

5

"I COULD HAVE STRANGLED HER," Kelly said. "That outfit ... " she made a fist " ... thankfully she and Liz are about the same size and build, so I had them swap clothes."

"Piercings too?" Don asked with a grin.

"Yep," Kelly said. "Put them into Liz myself." She let out a sigh. "I swear, if she shows up like that again for anything, even if it's just to hand over a check, I'm going to reach out, grab those titty rings through her shirt, and yank them right out."

"Ouch."

"Ouch is right, and I'm not kidding. I will yank

those suckers right out and then bill her for the bandaids."

"I believe you," he said. She was ruthless. "So, you win?"

"Of course I won. What kind of question is that?"

"Sorry. My bad."

"You?"

"Not yet."

She eyed him for a few seconds and then said, "What's wrong?"

"All I can think about when looking at him sitting in court is what if he had molested Belle and then got off on a technicality and now was suing me?"

Kelly didn't reply.

"I mean, Jesus Christ, what kind of fucked up world do we live in where a molester can not only get away with something like this but then go so far as to sue the victim's family?"

"Not exactly what you pictured yourself doing when you were in law school, is it?" Kelly asked.

"Not even remotely," he said. "You?"

"Eh, yes and no."

"Yes and no?"

"Most of my classmates seemed to picture themselves being the crusader defense attorney establishing precedent as they argued the biggest murder trials of the century. Not me. I always knew I would go into family law and never saw myself as a big-screen Hollywood creation that has no basis in reality."

"And the no part?"

"These cases that your mother has us work. It's like what the fuck is wrong with people? I always knew things could get crazy ugly with divorces, but Jesus Christ, they go way beyond anything I ever envisioned."

"Like my custody battle with Beth?" he asked.

"No, that's pretty straightforward. I'm talking like people who spend months fighting over a desk chair or a coffee mug."

"What? For real?"

"Yeah. And then there are the really ugly ones, like with that lady and the cat I told you about. Cases where they are just trying to hurt the other person."

"From Beth's point of view, that's what I'm trying to do. She thinks my wanting full custody of Belle is just my way of hurting her rather than protecting our daughter from an unstable mother."

"I can see her thinking that."

"And it's like I can't make her realize differently."

"Yeah."

A few seconds of silence.

"Any word on her mother?" Kelly asked.

"No, nothing," he said. "All of Beth's voicemails are just her being pissy with me about that cockpit photo of Jill, even though I had nothing to do with it."

A few more seconds of silence, then Kelly said, "Some interesting things involving her mother. Liz was doing background stuff for me and came across an old news story. Did you know there was a period when people thought she murdered her husband?"

"Buried him in the backyard," Don said with a nod. "Beneath her tomato plants."

"Yep. That seemed to be the most popular theory, though it doesn't seem like they ever found anything when digging up her veggie garden, or any other areas of the yard."

"They never found anything, period," Don noted. "The man pretty much vanished without a trace one day. They eventually declared him dead, which actually resulted in a pretty good size life insurance policy payout."

"Not an easy thing to accomplish."

Don didn't reply to that.

"She ever talk about it?"

"Who, Beth?"

"Yeah."

"Not really. That part of her childhood was a very touchy subject, and whenever it did come up, it always turned ugly."

"How so?"

"Beth pretty much blamed her mother for her father leaving. Apparently, his only real aspiration in life was to be an artist, but he could never break through with it. He was good, but not good enough to make a career out of it or anything. He wanted to try though, and felt that if he quit his job and started painting full time he would break through, but her mother was like no way, you have a family to support. Beth took this as her mother constantly demoralizing him, which eventually led to him abandoning them, striking off somewhere on his own where his art would be appreciated or something." He shook his head. "She was usually several drinks into things by this point, so it all became kind of unintelligible."

"Wow," she said. "Did he ever sell anything?"

"A piece here and there from time to time, but nowhere near enough to even consider the possibility that he could be a full-time artist."

"That's gotta be tough."

"Yeah."

"And not just for him, but for her too. Beth's mother. Can you imagine having to be the one to constantly tell someone they just aren't good enough to do what they dream of doing? It's like you want to be supportive of people and their dreams, but you also have to be realistic, especially if something like supporting a family hangs in the balance."

"Yeah," he said again. "Lucky for her, she wasn't the only one telling him he sucked."

"What do you mean?"

"Right before he left, he had his first art show. Nothing huge. Just at a local gallery in their little downtown area. But it drew a bit of a crowd, many of whom belittled the art within earshot of him."

"Oh jeez."

"And the critic at the local paper didn't hold back either. It was pretty brutal."

"Right before he left them?"

"Yeah."

"Huh."

"What?"

"Kind of odd. Lighting out like that to pursue an artistic dream right after being devastated by the public at a showing."

"Probably why no one knows his name. He took off to achieve his dream and totally failed because he really did suck."

6

. . .

"I THINK it was probably the milk," Mr. Flynn noted later that day.

"The milk?" Beth asked.

"That made Belle sick. It's expired by about a week."

"No!" she said, not in contradiction, but surprise. Horror was present as well. Both at the fact that she had forced Belle to finish the cereal after having been told it tasted funny, and at the fact the Mr. Flynn had discovered this and now could start making a list of things that made her an unfit mother. "I didn't even think to check that. It was here when we arrived and I just thought ... "

"It happens to the best of us," Mr. Flynn said.

Beth just shook her head.

"Trust me, I raised several of them, kids and grandkids, and the only sure thing I can say about raising kids, especially in an environment where so much other crazy stuff is happening, is this: shit happens."

Beth stared at him for a second and then burst out laughing.

He grinned.

"Shit happens," she said, wiping at her eyes. "That should be a mandatory subtitle for every child rearing book that is published."

Several more seconds came and went, Beth slowly feeling better about the Belle situation.

"So, how's your mother?" Mr. Flynn asked. "Is she talking yet?"

"No, not yet."

"Hmm."

"And they're not even sure if she ever will."

Mr. Flynn looked like he wanted to say something, but didn't.

Beth was silent as well.

Not long after that, he wished her a pleasant evening and started back to his house.

Beth watched him through the window, thoughts about him and her mother once again arriving.

What isn't he saying?

And why does he keep wanting to know if she is talking yet?

On the surface such a question seemed fairly innocent, but given her growing certainty that he and her mother had had some sort of relationship, she was starting to wonder if maybe his questions on her speaking wasn't so much one of asking about progress, but instead one of concern over what she might reveal in her confused mental state.

But why?

Even if the two had had some sort of illicit love affair going on, one that might have helped in driving her father away, what did it matter now? He was long since widowed, so it wasn't like her revealing something from the past would cause any problems now. It was all ancient history.

Or was it?

"Mommy?" a voice called.

"What is it, honey?" she asked as Belle entered the room, face exhausted and hair ruffled from sleeping.

"Are we going to get pizza?"

Beth nearly said no, but then instead asked, "Are you sure you're feeling okay for pizza?"

"I'm feeling a trillion percent better."

"A trillion percent?"

"Yes!"

"Okay, I guess we will get a pizza then."

"Yippy!"

With that, Beth opened her phone to see what places in the area offered delivery, thumb dismissing one place after another given the St. Louis Style displays on their pages that had the words *Provel Cheese* in their descriptions.

How anyone could love that stuff was a mystery to her, memories of constantly going hungry at birthday parties while growing up given the local popularity of such a disgusting creation arriving.

It was just nasty.

So nasty that Papa John's could actually be viewed as a tasty alternative to the St. Louis style monstrosity, though fortunately she didn't have to settle for that given that there were still several other independent places that recognized the need for quality pizza in the area.

7

"NOTHING MUCH. They just slapped my hand and reminded me of the airline's policy about how we conduct ourselves on social media," Jill said. "We are way too short staffed to have them firing me over something stupid like that."

"That's good," Beth replied.

"They did say I have to take down the photo, though, which really sucks because it's fucking hilarious."

"It is. I totally LOL'd back when you posted it."

Nothing followed for a few seconds, Beth thinking about the pizza box that was now in the fridge, contemplating grabbing another piece before she turned in for the night.

"I still can't believe they tried to fuck me like that," Jill said. "It really pisses me off."

"It's that fuck-buddy lawyer skank," Beth noted. "She's ruthless. It's not enough to win this thing. She wants to destroy me and anyone I'm friends with."

"Well, I can be ruthless too and now that she has messed with me, I'm totally going to fuck them all up."

"Maybe just let it go."

"Let it go?" Jill questioned. Then, apparently deciding to abuse Beth's eardrums, began singing the "Let it go" song from *Frozen*.

"Mercy!" Beth cried.

Jill chuckled.

"Seriously though," Beth said. "I'm not sure going after them is a good idea. It could escalate things."

"I'm pretty sure they are doing that on their own. I mean, just the fact that they started gunning for me at all is a sign. And now that they failed with that, I'm guessing they will try again with something else."

Beth didn't reply.

"But don't you worry about any of this. I'll take care of things up here while you just focus on your mother."

"Thanks," Beth said. Sadly, she didn't think it would be that easy to keep her separated from all the drama. After all, she was the main target in all this. They had simply focused on Jill due to her proximity and the fact that she was helping out with the lawyer fees."

"Anyway, I should probably call it a night. Got a LA and back tomorrow."

"Okay. Night."

"Night."

The call ended, Beth setting down the phone so that she could head to the fridge and grab that piece of pizza she had been thinking about.

Halfway to the kitchen she paused, her eyes settling on the Clue game that she and Belle had played while waiting for the pizza and then several times again after they had eaten their fill, Belle constantly wanting to do 'just one more game' as her bedtime loomed, then arrived.

Beth gave in twice.

Now, staring at the game, she thought about Mr. Flynn and the attic.

Something was up there.

Something he had wanted to check out.

Or was there?

Had he really gone up there to pretend to speak with a monster to help put Belle at ease? And then again to find a game?

No.

Something about her mother going up there while mentally confused had triggered concern from him, of this she was certain - especially given how often he had asked her about whether she was speaking yet.

But what?

Beth thought about going up there and looking around, but doing so at night seemed a bit chilling. Sure, there were lights up there, but even in the day they didn't do all that much, so at night ...

She shivered at the thought.

Eating a piece of pizza was a better idea and then turning in for the night.

8

TEN MINUTES LATER, Beth was opening the hallway door to the attic, her curiosity too much to put off until the morning.

Twelve steps awaited her, leading up to a landing that was encased in darkness.

A light switch was on the right.

She flipped it.

Darkness slithered away as light cut through it, but didn't disappear completely, waiting, ready to retake the area as soon as the light died out.

Stepping softly in hopes of not making any sounds that would wake up Belle, Beth went up the steps, a squeal from one of them sounding much louder than it probably was given her anxiety.

Belle didn't seem to notice.

Beth completed the ascent, eyes quickly noting that the light from the stairway barely went beyond the small landing. To add more light, she would need to walk about fifteen feet into the center of the attic and pull on a cord that dangled down.

It was a simple task, yet one that she didn't engage in right away. Instead, she scanned the darkness, eyes searching for things that the rational part of her mind knew would not be present.

There is no monster up here.

Not when it spends its night behind the wall in the bedroom.

She nearly chuckled at the thought, but then

realized there wasn't any amusement behind it and instead walked over to the light cord and gave it a tug.

Light.

Not much, but enough to look around a bit.

For what exactly, she did not know.

I'll know it when I see it.

Will I?

She really had no idea.

But look she did, eyes scanning all the various shelves, boxes, cloth-covered lumps of furniture, and all the old paintings her father had done and then ruined with a knife before leaving.

Nothing jumped out at her.

She scanned the same areas over and over again, each time coming away with nothing but an idea that she was being silly.

Mr. Flynn had been up here several times, but if it was for some odd, even nefarious reason, she would never be able to figure out what it was.

Not nefarious.

It couldn't be that.

But whatever it was, it had him concerned to the point of coming up here several times.

Does it even matter?

No.

She nearly turned around and headed back downstairs at that thought, but then realized the inner voice was wrong. It did matter. Not for any actionable reason, but simply for her. She wanted to know what had unfolded between her mother and Mr. Flynn.

Nothing would ever come of the information.

Even if they had been having an affair all those

years ago, it didn't matter because it wouldn't change anything.

Or would it?

No.

Nothing from the past ever changed the present.

Her mother would still be in the hospital, Don would still be fucking Kelly, and she would still be going through a divorce that she couldn't win.

Love letters?

Pictures?

Love letters and pictures?

Back when she was a kid, email wasn't used very much, so any illicit exchanges between the two would likely have been of a physical form, one that her mother could very well have stored somewhere up here. Or elsewhere in the house.

In fact, Mr. Flynn might have been searching for such items longer than she realized, her mother's growing dementia having made it so she would have no idea what he was doing during any visits he made.

And now, having failed to locate the stash anywhere else in the house, he had turned his attention to the attic, her mother's fall making him realize she might have stored everything up there.

The theory seemed so spot on that she pretty much accepted it as fact, one that she now wanted to prove by finding the letters and photos, her steps taking her all around the attic several more times as she searched everywhere, her mind completely obvious to the passage of time.

Nothing was found.

She opened boxes, pulled out drawers, removed

dust-cloths, looked under old furniture - all to no avail.

Exhaustion hit.

She took a seat on an old rocking chair by one of the windows, eyes closing for a second, and then opening again to stop the sleep that nearly overtook her.

Blink.
Eyes wide.
Blink.
Eyes wide.
Blink.
Eyes wide.

Over and over again she did this, trying to fight off the sleep enough so that she could get up and head back downstairs, this journey into the attic having been another fruitless endeavor in a life that seemed nothing but fruitless endeavors.

The kitty litter bags.

All of them were now stacked up against the wall.

Last time she had been up there, two of them had been to the side, her mother having simply dropped them upon the wooden floor as she completed her confused journey.

Why had Mr. Flynn stacked them?

Had he simply done it to straighten things up, or had he done it because he had forgotten that two of them had been dropped off to the side after he unstacked them for some reason?

No longer having to fight sleep given the new-found point of inquiry, she walked over to the litter bags to see why Mr. Flynn would have unstacked them, her hands pulling down the twenty pound bags one by one until that the area beneath the wall was completely clear.

Nothing.

No letters.

No pictures.

No tiny compartment in the wall that had been hidden behind the bags.

It was just the wooden floor.

Frustrated and feeling a bit foolish, Beth headed back downstairs, feet taking her all the way down to the first floor where she stood before the large liquor cabinet for several minutes, before heading to the couch where the pillow and blankets awaited her.

9

ROBERT FLYNN WAS WALKING to the bathroom for the third time that night when he saw the tiny square of light out beyond one of his hallway windows.

He paused for a second, staring, trying to make sense of the tiny square of light. And then it clicked.

A light was on up in an attic.

And not just any attic, but one that he had been up in himself earlier that day. One that Beth was now roaming around in for some reason during the midnight hour.

Concern arrived.

FIVE

I

"MOMMY, do you know why I didn't get scared last night?" Belle asked while waiting for breakfast.

"Why honey?" Beth asked, fighting off a yawn.

"Because I knew it was you making the thumping noises."

"Thumping noises?"

"Yep. Right above my head. Just like Mr. Flynn made the other day after I told him about how the monster scratches against the wall."

The toaster popped, the waffles ready, but Beth didn't plate them right away, her mind focused on picturing the bedroom in relation to the area of the attic where the kitty litter was.

Sure enough, that spot would have been right above the bedroom — right above the wall where the scratching sounds were coming from.

"Mommy, they're ready."

Beth shifted her focus back to the waffles, plating them and then serving them to Belle, who then went about trying to drown them in syrup,

Beth having to tell her *enough* twice before she stopped squeezing the bottle.

After that, she asked, "Did Mr. Flynn go up and start making the thumping noises right after you told him about the monster scratching on the wall?"

"Yep," Belle announced, syrup oozing from a forkful of waffle. "He marched right up and told the monster to stop trying to scare me." She popped the gooey mess of syrup smothered waffle into her mouth. "Is that what you were doing last night? Were you telling the monster not to scare me?"

"I was," she said.

Stop lying.

Just tell her there is no monster.

Beth ignored the inner voice and instead said, "And now I'm going back up there for a bit and you might hear more thumping noises, but you just stay here and keep eating, okay?"

"Okay."

Beth headed back up into the attic, the daylight from the various windows making the area seem like a completely different space than the one she had been in last night.

The kitty litter bags were still scattered where Beth had left them after dragging them from the pile and then away from the wall area, her mind now asking herself why Mr. Flynn would have gone straight up to this very spot to move the bags of litter after being told about the scratching sounds.

Several seconds came and went without answer as she stared at the floor, frustration once again arriving.

. . .

"WHY DON'T you just ask him?" Jill suggested.

"It would be awkward," Beth said.

"Why?"

"I don't know. *Hey, Mr. Flynn, why did you move all those bags of kitty litter after Belle mentioned the scratching sounds in the wall? Was it because you and my mom were having sex when I was a kid?*"

"Well yeah, if you ask it like that it would be awkward. Especially if they weren't having sex at all and he simply went up there because he is a nice old man that wanted to try to ease the terror that Belle is experiencing."

"But why go right to the kitty litter bags?"

"Are you sure he really did?"

"I know he moved them around for some reason and that it was right after Belle mentioned the scratching sounds."

"According to Belle."

"She wouldn't lie about that."

"Not saying that, just that you're basing this on the idea that Belle's stated timing for everything is spot on."

"I think she is being pretty spot on with it."

"How?"

"I can't really explain it. You just have to trust me. It's a mother thing."

"Okay," Jill said.

Beth could feel Jill rolling her eyes all the way up in Chicago.

"Have the scratching sounds stopped?" Jill asked.

"What do you mean?"

"Well, you said that it seemed like maybe the wind was rattling something in there, like through the old thin walls. So maybe thinking the same thing, Mr. Flynn went up there and did something to stop the scratching sounds."

"Like what?"

"I don't know. What's it like up there? Is the floor finished all the way to the wall or is there an opening that he could have reached through down into the wall and grabbed whatever nest was making the scratching sounds?"

"Huh, you know, I can't really say. There is a floor up there, actual floorboards that are solid so that you can walk around and whatnot as if it's an actual room, but I'm not certain that it's flush to the wall." A pause. "Let me go look."

"I'll be here."

"It's a cell phone," Beth said with a laugh. "You'll be with me."

Jill made her own chuckle sound.

Beth headed back up into the attic, a sense of relief that she hadn't stacked the kitty litter up against the wall arriving.

"You know what? There is a tiny bit of a gap between the wall and the floorboards."

"Enough to reach down into the wall through."

"No, but now that I'm looking at the final floorboard that is across that area, it doesn't look like it has any nails in it."

"See if you can pull it up."

Beth knelt down and put her fingers through the tiny gab so that she could grip the floorboard, which popped right out.

"You were right," Beth said, staring at the large gap in the floor. "The board came right up and now

I could totally reach down there between the walls if I wanted to."

"Mystery solved," Jill said.

"Mystery solved," Beth repeated as if in agreement, though now she wondered how had he known the floorboard would come up?

Did he know?

Or had he just discovered it?

And once it came up ...

She looked around to see if there was anything he could have used to reach down with, the distance from the attic floor to whatever it was that had been causing scratching noises way too far for an arm.

Or was it?

She tried peeking down through the opening to see, but couldn't get a good look given how low the roofline was in this area. One thing she did note: no insulation.

An oversight during construction? she wondered. *Or normal for the age of this house?*

Jill was saying something that Beth didn't catch, a brief statement of, "Hang on a sec," leaving Beth's lips as she got down onto her knees once again and then lowered herself all the way down so that she could reach into the wall to see what was down there.

Nothing, nothing, nothing, and then something.

It was big and had an odd feel to it, almost a rough leather-like texture. Other parts were clumpy and gave off a tangled feeling, one that initially made her think *spider web* before noting it was too clumped together and too thick for that.

No images of what it could be entered into her mind as she explored the object. It was something big, though. Of that, she had no doubt. Something big that had no business being within the walls.

"What do you think it is?" Jill eventually asked once Beth returned to the phone conversation and mentioned what she had just felt.

"I have no idea, and I can't really get a good look, not unless I pry up another board and get my face right up against the floor to look down."

"Do it!"

"What? Pull up another board. This next one is pretty solid."

"So, pry it up. It's your house."

Not quite, but ...

"Maybe I can get a picture. Hang on a second." She switched over to the camera mode of her phone, thumbed on the flash and then carefully lowered it down, an inner voice saying *Don't drop it!* over and over again.

Several pictures were taken, her finger holding down the photo button.

"Okay, let's see if I can tell what it is," Beth said once she had the phone back out and away from the opening.

"I'm on pins and needles," Jill replied.

Beth opened the photos and started scrolling, the first several being too blurry.

A clear one appeared.

Beth gasped and dropped the phone.

3

"BETH?" a tiny voice asked. "Beth?"

Beth blinked several times, her mind trying to deny what her eyes had seen.

It couldn't be. No. Not possible. Yet ...

"Beth? Are you okay?"

Not only did she know what it was her eyes had seen in the photo - what it was that was stuck down there in the wall — she knew who it was as well. It all came together in an instant, the sudden understanding of everything slamming into her as if it possessed a physical form.

"Beth?"

She picked up the phone and said, "Hey, sorry."

"What happened?"

"Dropped my phone," she said, surprised at how calm her voice was.

"That bad, huh?" Jill asked.

"What?"

"The picture of the thing in the walls. It made you drop your phone."

"Yeah," Beth said, forcing out a laugh.

"Well, what was it?"

"A giant spider web with a huge half eaten rat all webbed up," she lied.

"Ugh! No! No! No! And you were touching it."

"Yeah," Beth said, looking at her hand. Disgust present.

"That's horrible."

Beth didn't reply, still staring at her hand.

"Shit, what kind of spiders do you have down there?"

"What do you mean?"

"If it webbed up a rat, that must be fucking huge."

"Oh yeah," she said, switching back to the lie,

"we get all kinds of nasty things down here. Snakes, spiders, it's like ... " she didn't finish, unsure what else to compare it to.

"And they're in your house," Jill said. "Jesus Christ. And here I was thinking of coming down there to visit and comfort you."

"You still could," Beth said, knowing Jill wouldn't.

"I can't even watch *Arachnophobia* so no way am I going to live it." Then, after a few seconds. "Do you think he killed it?"

Beth felt her heart speed up. "Who?"

"The old guy. Mr. Flynn. Do you think he realized there was a giant spider in the walls and killed it?"

"Oh. Um. Yeah, probably."

"That's good at least."

"Yeah. Hey, I think I better go so I can wash my hand from touching that and then get to the hospital to see my mother."

Mother.

Mr. Flynn.

Had he helped her?

With the killing or simply in figuring out how to hide the body after the fact?

All while I was at school?

A shudder raced through her. Not just at the idea of what her mother and Mr. Flynn had done, but at the realization that for several years she had been sleeping right up against a wall with her father's body behind it.

4

. . .

"YOUR MOTHER IS DRIVING ME CRAZY," Kelly said while plopping herself down on his office sofa, frustration clearly present.

"How so?" he asked, eyes noting how her skirt had ridden up to the point of making garters visible, a sight that momentarily made him once again contemplate trying to breach the friend-zone perimeter even though he knew it would never work.

"She has started demanding updates on everything and doesn't seem pleased with our progress. She even chewed me out for not fighting their request for a continuance due to her mother's accident. It's like *what the fuck?*"

"Jesus. I'll talk to her," Don said. "Get her to ease up."

Kelly shifted herself a bit so that her arm now cushioned the back of her head.

"What exactly does she have against her?" she asked.

"Who?"

"Your mother. With Beth. What happened between those two?"

"Honestly, nothing."

"Nothing?"

"Yeah. She simply hated Beth from day one and I never could figure out why. And she never hid it either. Always belittling her and whatnot anytime all of us were together. And then claiming she got pregnant just to trap me. Stuff like that."

"Wow."

"Yeah. And then she started saying Beth was trying to drive a wedge between us."

"Was that when Beth convinced you to start your own practice?"

"Yeah." He shook his head. "Which I guess I

can totally see as being very wedge-like from my mother's point of view."

Kelly didn't reply to that.

"And in the end, I guess my mother was right about Beth and how I should never have married her. I mean, drinking before her turn with a car pool. Almost killing our daughter and all those kids."

"You mentioned she was going to AA and all that before the incident," Kelly said.

"Yeah. She had made a lot of progress too. I was really proud of her. Seemed like she had finally turned things around this time."

"That's tough."

"I had even suggested we have a party to celebrate her success, but she didn't want — "

A knock echoed on the doorframe, his secretary looking in, disapproval present on her face when she saw Kelly sprawled on the sofa, a comment about his new client having arrived with her daughter.

"Thanks," he said.

Kelly pushed herself up, smoothed out her skirt and slipped her foot back into a heel that had fallen to the floor. "I best be off," she said.

"Want to get some dinner later?" he asked.

"Dinner?" she asked, clearly caught off guard.

"Yeah, to ... um ... go over stuff with the case."

"Can't tonight. Got a prior engagement.

"Oh. Okay. No worries."

She eyed him for a moment before slipping out through the open doorway and heading to her own office.

Shit, he said to himself. *She saw right through that and totally shot me down.*

Or did she?

He shook the thoughts away and then let his secretary know he was ready for his next client. It was a mother daughter duo; the mother engaging his services on behalf of her daughter who had gotten into a fight with a drive-thru employee over something involving a beverage, the end result being that the daughter had put out one of the employee's eyes while trying to hit her in the face.

5

BETH STARED at her mother for a long time while standing in the small ICU room, dozens of questions echoing in her mind - questions that could not be asked at that time.

She wanted to know why.

Why had they killed her father?

Had something been going on that she had been oblivious to? Something terrible? Abuse of some kind? Like with the drunk husband in that Stephen King movie with Kathy Bates and the eclipse?

Or was it something else?

Something mundane?

Like the stupid reasons that are uncovered in episodes of *Forensic Files*?

Was Mr. Flynn really involved?

Yes.

He had to be.

How else would he have known what was causing the scratching sounds whenever the wind blew following the earthquake, and where to go in the attic to try to put a stop to it so that she wouldn't eventually investigate it herself?

Is that really what he had done?

Yes.

It had to be.

Belle had mentioned the scratching to him, which had worried him given that he knew what would happen if Beth eventually opened the wall to see what it was, so he went up to silence it before it became too big a deal.

In fact, he had probably been worried prior to that, the incident with the kitty litter on the stairs making him realize her mother's mind was not where it needed to be to keep a secret. If she was confused enough to start having kitty litter brought to the house thinking she still had cats, what else might she mention?

Had she really fallen on her own?

What if Mr. Flynn had actually pushed her down the stairs and then left her there to die? Maybe after learning from his grandson about how she had asked him to buy kitty litter for her?

It was this latter thought that had kept her from having Mr. Flynn babysit that day, Belle having come with her to the hospital.

She would not leave her daughter with that man again.

She didn't care how old he was; how charming he seemed.

Nope.

Even if he had not actually been involved in the murder and had simply come over to help hide the body after the fact, she would not allow him in the house or near her daughter.

So many questions, but no answers.

Not yet.

Maybe not ever.

And no one to talk to about it.

Unless ...

Could she talk to Jill?

Could she be all like: *'Hey, guess what, my mother killed my father when I was a kid and hid his body behind the wall, and the earthquake the other day must have shifted the body a bit so that it started scratching against the wall whenever a gust of wind hit the house.'*

How would Jill react to that?

Actually, she was pretty sure she knew exactly what Jill would say. *'Is there enough room in there for Don?'*

Nothing followed after that, her mind going completely blank for a while. Not because of how accurate the thought was when it came to things Jill would say, but because of how she actually started to wonder about the possibility.

Was there room for him in there?

And his little fuck buddy lawyer friend?

Or him and his mother?

Or just his mother?

No! No! No!

Blanking out her mind, she took one last look at her own mother before heading back to the waiting area where Belle was busy with a coloring book a nurse had found for her, a need to sit down suddenly overwhelming her.

"Mommy?" Belle asked, concerned.

Nothing.

"Are you okay?" Belle pressed.

"I'm fine, sweetie."

Satisfied, Belle went back to her coloring book.

Is there room ...

Stop!

A few seconds later ...

The wall is large so there would be space on either side ...

Stop!

And then ...

If they were dismembered, the pieces could just be dropped down on either side of her father ...

Beth actually covered her ears at this thought, as if that somehow would shield her from hearing the inner voice.

It didn't.

Instead, she eventually stopped the thoughts with a simple inner statement about how she would never be able to get away with it. Not in this day and age. Not when everyone would wonder what had happened to her husband and the fuck-buddy lawyer friend.

Questions would lead investigators into the house and once there they would be like: 'Holy hell, what is that smell?'

After that, they would tear the house apart looking for the source, eventually finding the fresh bodies rotting away alongside the old leathery body of her father.

Mother and daughter, both in jail for murder, all while Belle ended up in foster care.

That's better than where she will end up once Don wins custody of her.

No.

Yes.

It was.

Beth knew that Don didn't really want custody of Belle. If he did, he wouldn't be looking at boarding schools overseas. She was just something to win. Something to take away in an effort to hurt her in the divorce.

She couldn't let that happen.

Not to her daughter.

Never.

6

SHOULD I CONFRONT HIM? Beth asked herself, her mind picturing Mr. Flynn sitting at the kitchen table, a look of surprise and horror on his face when she mentioned the body within the wall.

What would his reaction be?

Given his age, Beth didn't think he would be able to do anything to her, not unless he had a gun secretly tucked away.

No.

Somehow she knew he wouldn't have one, and that he wouldn't react with violence of any kind.

She also knew she wouldn't confront him.

Not yet.

Not right away.

Not without thinking things over very carefully.

"Mommy? Can I have more Coke?"

Beth blinked a few times to bring herself back to the current moment, the hospital cafeteria coming back into focus around her.

"You drank that entire thing already?" Beth asked.

"It was mostly ice."

Beth knew that had not been the case given that

she had filled it herself while at the beverage station, but let that go.

Not long after that, Belle had a fresh cup of Coke, one that Beth took a few large sips from, which earned a frantic "Don't drink it all!" from Belle, who seemed genuinely concerned by the potential outcome.

They headed back upstairs to the ICU waiting area.

"Can I see grandma too?" Belle asked.

"Not yet, honey," she said.

Belle was too young for the ICU area — as a visitor.

Beth couldn't see her mother either, though not because of age. Something had happened while they were downstairs eating; something bad; something that required her to be rushed to an operating room.

Nothing beyond that was revealed to her, likely because they really didn't know anything themselves at this point.

7

"IT COULD BE ANYTHING," Beth said into the phone, pacing, second cigarette of the hour already going, her steps frequently taking her into the No Smoking Within 15 Feet of This Entrance zone. "At her age and with her injuries ... " her voice faded without concluding the statement.

"Fuck," Jill said. Then, after a few seconds, "I'm coming down there."

"What? No, no, you don't have to do that," Beth said.

"I want to," Jill said. "You shouldn't be alone through all this."

"Seriously, I'm fine."

"Are you sure? It might not seem like you need someone, but once I'm there, you might realize how helpful it is."

Beth knew Jill was right, and honestly, having Jill there would be really helpful. But she didn't want anyone else in the house. Not yet. Not until she fully processed her discovery and what her next steps would be.

No ...

She didn't want her mind going down that path again. It wouldn't work. The moment Don went missing, everyone would be looking at her and there would be no way to hide it.

"How is Belle doing?" Jill asked.

"Belle?" Beth questioned. "She's totally fine, except ... "

"Except what?" Jill asked.

"I'm going to lose her."

"You don't know that."

"I do. Nothing I say or do will convince that judge to let me have custody of her, not after skidding into that crossing guard with a car full of kids while there was alcohol in my system."

"That's such bullshit," Jill said.

"I just have to face the facts," Beth replied.

"No, I mean the whole drinking thing. I just don't buy it. There was something fishy about all that."

"I wish."

"Seriously, his mother probably paid off the

cops or something to make you fail the breathalyzer."

"It was a blood test, not a breathalyzer."

"Okay, the hospital then. Or the lab. Someone."

"Maybe," Beth muttered.

"No maybe about it. You weren't drinking that morning. Not before a carpool. And not after being sober for so long."

"I don't know."

"Yes, you do know. You insisted upon it. And I know you. Even Don tried to figure it out. I mean, he had those tests run to see if your body produced alcohol on its own or something from sugar."

"And it didn't."

"Which is why I have always said there was something fishy about all that. I mean, why even draw your blood to test for alcohol while you were in the hospital? Who suggested they do that? You didn't even have enough in your system for it to be a DUI so no one would have claimed you were acting drunk while picking up their kids."

"It doesn't really matter anymore."

Jill didn't reply to that, likely because she realized Beth was right. She had gone to jail after that, the judge showing no mercy on her given her past history with alcohol, and Don had filed for divorce. If his mother had done something to make that all happen, then she had succeeded.

Jill was right, though.

She hadn't been drinking.

And to this day, she had no idea why there had been alcohol in her system.

Or where all the bottles of vodka had come from.

"He is going to win this thing," Beth continued. "He'll win and I will never get to see Belle again."

"You'll still get to see her," Jill said.

"No. Once he gets full custody, they're going to send her off to a boarding school."

"What? Are you sure?"

"Don emailed me info on the schools to see if I have a preference."

"That motherfucker."

"Yeah."

Jill was silent for a long time after that, and then asked, "Anything I can do?"

"No. Nothing anyone can do at this point."

"And you're sure you don't want me to come down?"

"Not right now."

"Okay, but just remember, I'm here for you. Anything you need. Day or night. And if you change your mind and want me there, I'm there. If you want to simply be alone, I totally understand. Money, food, a hired thug to go beat up Don. Anything."

Beth chuckled. "That last one ... I'm so tempted."

"Fuck, I might just do that one for me."

Another chuckle.

"Or maybe just stink bomb his office."

"Now that is something I can totally get behind," Beth said.

"And your house, since you're not there right now."

"He'll be living in stink for days!"

The smell!

How did Mom and Mr. Flynn get rid of the smell?

"How long does it take for that to go away?" she asked.

"A stink bomb? I have no idea. But remember that time I thought it would be a good idea to try to cook fish so that I could start being healthy again, and then forgot to take the trash out before heading to LA and it stunk up the place so bad that the police were called to do a wellness check by the idiots upstairs."

"Ha! Yes!"

"Well, I eventually used coffee grounds to get rid of it."

"Coffee grounds?"

"Yeah. You burn the shit out of them in a skillet on the stove. That in itself stinks too, which pissed off the neighbors again, but a burned coffee smell is better than a rotting fish smell. And it somehow absorbs it or something, so once the burned coffee smell was gone, so was the rotting fish smell."

"Hmm, interesting."

Had her mother ever done that?

She couldn't remember any burned coffee smells in the house. In fact, the only smell she really remembered was the pungent Arm and Hammer from the kitty litter. That stuff was strong, especially since her mother made her keep a litter box in her bedroom, and constantly hounded her about changing it. More so than any of the other boxes in the house, which always puzzled her because the one in her room seemed to be one the cats didn't particularly care to use.

And it didn't matter how far from her bed she put the box, she always felt like she was living in a cloud of Arm and Hammer, the scent making it almost impossible to be in her room.

Ohhhh my god!

Was that why her mother had given her two kittens that day?

So that house would always be filled with the Arm and Hammer scent from the litter boxes?

Would that be enough to mask the smell of a body rotting behind the wall? Behind her wall?

And then it clicked.

Everything.

Why they always seemed to go through kitty litter like crazy when she was a kid, and why her mother had been carrying bags of it up into the attic after starting to go senile.

"I better run," Beth said, stubbing out her cigarette against the brick wall. "I left Belle with a nurse who is probably running out of patience so that I could grab a smoke."

"Okay, keep me posted."

"Will do."

"Hang in there."

"Thanks."

Beth tucked the phone away but didn't head back into the hospital. Instead, she took a seat on a bench so that she could think things over for a bit, her mind having ventured into a dark place once again - one that should have sent her bolting back to the light of the sane, normal world it usually resided in.

Instead, she stayed in the dark place, exploring it, seeing what possibilities it had to offer her.

SIX

I

"MOMMY, WHY IS IT CALLED MONSTER?" Belle asked.

"I don't know, honey," Beth said after grabbing several cans of the energy drink and starting toward the counter.

"Is it like those juice boxes at Halloween?"

"Maybe."

"Am I going to get to trick-or-treat this year?"

"Of course."

"Yay! Last year Daddy wouldn't let me."

"He didn't?" Beth asked, caught off guard.

"He said it was still too dangerous because of the cobra virus."

Anger flared up.

Beth had been in jail during the last two Halloweens, the first of which had been at the tail end of the Covid-19 pandemic (or the cobra virus as Belle always called it), so Belle still had not been able to go trick-or-treating. But last year things had been better, and there would have been no reason why Don should not have taken her. No good reason. And the fact that he had told her it was due to the virus again ... she didn't know why, but that really pissed her off.

He doesn't want to be a father.

Never did.

And once he has full custody of her ...

Off to one of the boarding schools.

No!

She could not let him win this thing.

And the only way to beat him was ...

No!

It won't work.

It will work.

Back and forth these statements went as she purchased the energy drinks, then while in the Uber on their way home, and then while back in the house.

"Honey," she said after getting Belle settled with a jigsaw puzzle she had found in the attic. "I have to go into the garage for a while."

"Okay," Belle said, fingers starting to turn over all the pieces so that they were image side up.

"After that, we will order some dinner."

"Okay."

Oh to be a kid again, Beth thought. *Not a care in the world beyond the jigsaw puzzle, mind totally oblivious to all the drama unfolding between her parents.*

Is she really oblivious to it?

Was I?

Beth found herself dwelling upon this as she headed out into the garage, her mind eventually concluding that no, she had not been oblivious to it, which meant that Belle probably wasn't either, but that she had never realized the full extent of it, which hopefully would be the same for Belle.

If I do go through with this ...

Nothing followed for several seconds as her body got into her mother's car.

Deep breath.

If it turns on ...

She twisted the key in the ignition.

The engine came to life without issue.

She let it run while contemplating things.

Chicago and back during the night, all while Belle was asleep.

But if she wakes up and discovers an empty house ...

Some Benadryl right before bed?

Mixed in with some ice cream.

Like I used to do when she was younger and refused to go to sleep.

Four hours there, four hours back, and however long it took to get Don's body into the car and then out of the car and into the attic.

All while chugging one Monster after another to stay awake.

It seemed very doable.

The fact that there were no tolls on I-55 between here and the house made things even better, since that meant nothing would document her journey.

She would have to stop for gas at some point, though, and gas stations meant cameras.

Fuck.

There was no way around that.

The car could make it there on one tank of gas, but not there and back, and if she filled up anywhere along the way, there would be a record of her journey, which the police would eventually uncover.

Fuck! Fuck! Fuck!

She turned the car off and stepped out of it.

Mr. Flynn was waiting for her beyond the garage, his unexpected presence catching her off guard.

2

"LIZ. What are you still doing here?" Kelly asked, surprised to see Liz hunched over a file given that she and her girlfriend Lacy were supposed to be going to a party that evening. One that Liz had been talking about for weeks.

"Just looking into something Don's mother called about," Liz said. "Only there is nothing in any of the files about it."

"What was it?"

"She wanted to know why we weren't using any of the drinking complaints that were called in about Beth in the weeks prior to the accident as part of our argument about why Don should have full custody of Belle."

"What complaints?"

"That's what I said, which earned me quite the earful on how we're not doing our due diligence on this, and that Beth is going to take Don to the cleaners, which is total bullshit." Liz let out a heavy sigh. "Anyway, I've been going over everything from all the files pertaining to the accident and trial, and put in some calls, but there is literally nothing about any complaints being called in about her back then. Not in the police files, not during the trial itself, nothing. And when I put in a call to the hospital to see if I could talk to anyone who worked with Beth back then, I was bounced around from one department to the next for about forty-five minutes before someone disconnected me."

"You know what? Don't worry about any of this. I'll look into this myself."

"Are you sure?" Liz asked.

"Totally," Kelly said. "Go have fun with Lacy."

"It's just with us being chewed out about the continuance earlier and now this ..."

"Liz," Kelly said. "It's all good. She is just being a bitch. And if any shit does hit the fan, I'll handle it."

Liz stood where she was, unease still apparent, finger toying with her sleeve.

"Go. Have. Fun!"

"Thanks," Liz said, a huge grin appearing.

A curtsy followed, one that brought a smile to Kelly's face.

Liz was cute.

And fun.

As was her significant other, Lacy, the three of them having gotten together many times after Liz's accidental reveal of the interesting kinky lifestyle the two shared.

Liz was also a hard worker and knew what she was doing when it came to digging stuff up, so if she couldn't find anything on any mysterious complaints that were supposedly filed back when Beth worked as an ICU nurse in the city, then there probably was nothing to find.

And yet, Don's mother thought there was.

Enough to chew Liz out about it.

Odd.

3

"SHE'S FINALLY STARTING to come around," Beth lied.

"Really?" Mr. Flynn replied.

"Yeah. We were able to talk for a long time before she drifted off."

"That's wonderful."

Is it? she wondered, trying to gauge his true thoughts. "She's a bit confused, though. Kept drifting into random topics."

"Well, that's to be expected after a trauma like that. It will take some time, but her mind will sort everything out."

"I hope so," she said. "Especially since one of the topics she keeps drifting into is about my father."

Mr. Flynn didn't react to that, which in itself seemed a reaction, because it probably meant he was trying not to react.

"I hate to see her reliving the hurt of him abandoning her over and over again," she added.

"That's gotta be tough."

"Yeah. It's kind of making me dwell on those days as well, which I really don't want to do." She shook her head. "It was bad enough the idea of being abandoned, but then when everyone started to suggest that she killed him ... it was unbearable."

No reaction.

"Especially at that age. I mean, being a kid is hard, but then when all the other kids latch on to the idea that your mother is a killer that buried your father somewhere in the backyard." She paused for effect. "Well, no one ever wanted to spend the night at Beth's house after that."

"Kids are cruel. Always have been, always will be."

"Adults too."

"True."

"It's human nature, I guess."

A slight nod. Then, "You know she didn't kill him, right?"

Beth stared at him, unsure how to respond.

"All that stuff people said, all those theories, total nonsense," he added.

"I've been telling myself that for years," she said. "And I'd really like to believe it, but …"

He waited.

"Sometimes it's just hard," she added.

"Well, just put all of that out of your mind and know that despite any problems they had, she loved him and you, and always wanted what was best for you."

How was killing him and hiding his body behind the very wall I slept next to best for me?

No answers arrived in her mind.

And he clearly would not start down that route of explanation without prompting.

"I just don't understand him leaving like that," she said, shaking her head.

"It was very unexpected," he replied.

"I don't mean the act of him leaving itself. I don't understand the way he left."

Mr. Flynn gave her a look, clearly not grasping what she was alluding to.

"He took nothing with him. No clothes, none of

his art books or supplies, nothing of value whatsoever."

"Maybe he figured it would be too heavy during his walk to the train station," Mr. Flynn suggested.

"But why destroy all his paintings? He slashed every single one of them with a knife, all except the one I had in my room. And then headed off to pursue his art career unencumbered by family? That just doesn't make sense to me. Not if he felt he was good enough to strike out on his own and live off his artwork."

Mr. Flynn spread his hands and said, "Your father was not himself that week. Not after that art show, and especially not after reading that review."

Beth nodded.

"Actually, he had not been himself for quite some time. The ups and downs, the mood swings. You might have been too young to remember all this, but he would sometimes go weeks without painting anything, and then without warning it would be all he did when home, ignoring you and your mother, forgoing food and sleep, sometimes skipping work, almost like he was possessed."

Another nod. "His periods of inspiration. Whenever he finally caught hold of it, we would have to give him his space so that he didn't lose it or else the paintings would be busts."

Mr. Flynn shook his head.

"What?" she asked.

"I was just remembering one of those moments of inspiration. It was before you were born, during the Fourth of July. Your parents had just bought the house a few months earlier and were having a barbecue in the backyard. No formal invites or anything, just kind of a come one, come all sort of thing for everyone on the street so we could all meet them." He paused for a few seconds. "Anyway, some early fireworks were shot off out in the field while your father was grilling a batch of burgers. As the fireworks concluded, the smell of the burgers burning caught our attention and when we turned to look at what had happened, we realized your father was no longer there. He was just gone. I guess the airburst of the fireworks had inspired him or something, because he had raced inside to start painting. Your mother tried to get him to come back out, but he would not budge, not until he finished the painting."

Beth waited to see if anything else was going to follow, and when nothing did, asked, "Your point?"

"No point really, I guess," he admitted. "It's just that he dropped everything — abandoned everything if you will — to go work on a painting because of that sudden burst of inspiration."

"And you're saying that is pretty much what he did later to me and my mother, just on a more outrageous scale?"

"Well, yes, I suppose. But also I just wanted to point out that this was really humiliating for your mother given that this was the first neighborhood event they were hosting and though it wasn't a formal thing by any means, she was still really embarrassed by it. That he could just drop everything like that without warning. And then it started happening more and more, eventually getting to the point where they couldn't host anything, and no one really ever wanted to invite them to anything because there was no telling if your father would actually show up, or if he would suddenly leave during it, often dragging your mother home with him because if she refused to leave he would cause a huge scene and then sometimes just drive away without her."

Is he building up to trying to justify her having killed him? she wondered.

"These sudden bursts of inspiration, as he liked to call them, were one extreme, whereas the other extreme was almost like the complete opposite of inspiration. A de-inspiration if there is such a thing where he would decide he was no good and sometimes go so far as to toss out all his art stuff, destroy all the stuff he had worked on, and vow to never again pick up a brush."

Beth tried to remember one of those moments, but couldn't bring up anything specific within her mind. "I don't remember anything like that ever happening. Before him leaving, that is."

"Hmm, those might have been easier for your mother to shield you from."

Shield me?

"He had other odd moments, too."

"What do you mean?"

"Do you remember the Bob Ross incident?" he asked.

"Bob Ross? Is he the guy with the afro?"

"Yeah."

"I know about him, but not about any incident."

"You were still pretty young."

"What happened?"

"Your father hated Bob Ross. He didn't think his art was good at all and would become angry at how popular he was, and how effortlessly he painted things without any real plan of action. Stumbling upon one of his painting shows while flipping through the channels, or just seeing his stuff somewhere out in public, had the ability to enrage your father. It was bizarre. Like a switch being flipped. And then one day while in an art store, he saw a Bob Ross display and completely lost it while in the store. It got so bad that the police were called. Thankfully, no charges were filed, but your father was banned from the store, which is why your mother was always the one that went out to buy his art supplies." A pause. "I think this is why your mother was so fearful of these moments, because they could be very destructive to the point of violence, whereas the inspiration moments were simply productive to the extreme — though sometimes to the determent of other commitments."

"So you're saying he probably was in one of these destructive mindsets following the art show and that review, destroyed all his stuff, but then bounced into the inspiration mindset and took off to pursue his art career."

"No. I don't think he bounced back into an inspiration mindset. I think his leaving was part of a de-inspiration, self-destructive mindset, one that was far more extreme than any previous ones had been - even the Bob Ross incident."

Beth didn't know what to say to this, mostly because she knew he was lying. Her father hadn't left as part of any self-destructive mindset.

"Of course, I'm no expert in such things. Neither was your mother. This is why she tried so hard to get him to go see someone, but he wouldn't. I think because at some point when he was younger his parents had made him see someone who put him on some sort of medication that helped prevent the self-destructive mindsets, but also prevented the extreme inspiration mindsets, which he didn't want to be without."

"Mommy?" a voice called.

Startled, Beth turned toward the house.

"Sounds like you are being summoned," Mr. Flynn said. "I should head back."

Beth nodded.

"Let me know when she is able to have visitors. I'd really like to go see how she is doing."

"Will do."

She watched as he started the journey back toward his own house, his steps slow and carefully placed so as not to slip and fall.

Did he really help kill my father?

Seeing him today, it seemed unthinkable given that a simple breeze could probably topple him, but two decades ago he would have been in much better condition and though she couldn't really remember his physique all that much, she was pretty sure that killing her father and getting the body up into the attic wouldn't have been an issue. Especially with her mother lending a hand.

All while I was at school.

And then they went out to get me some kittens.

She wondered whose idea that had been, which eventually led to her wondering if the whole thing had been premeditated. Had they been planning the murder for several weeks, months even, the idea of using kitty litter to mask the smell something they had worked out in advance as opposed to on the spot?

All because of his mental swings?

All because they feared he really would quit his job and try to paint full time?

Or because her mother wanted to be rid of the

stress of his swings, but needed to be rid of him in such a way that she would eventually get a life insurance payout?

"Mommy?" Belle called once again.

"Coming!" she shouted back.

4

BETH STARED at the gap between the attic wall and the floor, her hands having pulled up a few more floorboards so that she had a nice large opening, her father's body clearly visible in the beam of light from the flashlight app on her phone.

Time ticked by as her mind theorized how things had unfolded all those years ago, her thinking being that they had likely pried up several floorboards like this as well to get the body down between the walls and then nailed all but the one closest to the wall back in place, thus allowing for ease of access when pouring kitty litter down there to absorb fluids and the smell.

For ten years ...

Beth figured this timeframe out after noting the expiration dates on the old bags of kitty litter that had been collecting dust for years prior to the new bags being added following the mental confusion that had caused her mother to start reliving the past.

Ten years of constantly pouring kitty litter down between the walls.

Did it really take that long before the body reached a state where there would be no noticeable smell? Or had it simply been that long before her mother realized such action was no longer necessary, the smell likely having ceased years earlier without her realizing it given how well the kitty litter had worked?

I will soon find out.

No.

Yes.

Only if I can figure out a way to get to Chicago and back on one tank of gas.

She bent down to put the floorboards back in place, but paused, her eyes noting something she had not seen before in the photos she had taken when first discovering the body.

It looked like a rope.

One that dangled halfway down the body, the end badly frayed.

Beth got down onto the floor and then leaned over the opening so she could reach in and see if the rope was around the neck, her fingers instantly feeling the old, worn threads.

A noose.

They hanged him.

That explained why there was no blood for the police to find when they briefly looked over the house to see if the story of his having abandoned them checked out, their eyes having failed to find any evidence of foul play.

No blood.

No body.

No blood.

No body.

No blood.

No body.

On and on this went, almost like a mantra, only with her mind picturing the house up in Chicago rather than the attic she was currently in, all while her hands replaced the floorboards.

5

BETH WAS in the attic again.

Robert Flynn could see this from the window in his old study, which gave him the best view of the house, the light within the attic window like a beacon in the night now whenever it was turned on.

She knows.

And yet, she hadn't said anything.

Why?

No answers arrived.

One thing he did know, he needed to talk to her about all this. He needed to make her understand what had happened that night after her father saw the stupid review of his artwork in the paper. He needed to make her understand why they had decided to put her father's body between the walls rather than calling the police.

SEVEN

I

"COMPLAINTS?" Don asked, yawning, Kelly's sudden appearance at his front door that morning having obviously pulled him out of bed. "You mean the ones called into the hospital?"

"I guess," Kelly said. "Were they about her drinking?"

"Yeah, but ..." he shook his head "... I don't understand, why are you looking into those?"

"Your mother. She chewed Liz out for us not using these mysterious complaints in our arguments, which totally caught both of us off guard because we had never heard of any complaints. And there literally is nothing in any of the files anywhere about them."

"No, there wouldn't be because nothing ever came of them."

"Explain."

"Not really all that much to explain," he said. "For like three or four weeks someone kept calling the hospital to complain that they could smell alcohol on Beth's breath."

"What did the hospital do?"

"They looked into things a bit but could find no evidence that she was drinking while on the job. And the idea that someone could smell it on her breath given all the PPE that was being used seemed a bit unrealistic."

"Wow. What did Beth say?"

"She was a bit dumbfounded by the whole thing, though at one point she did suggest that maybe it was the hand sanitizer. That stuff has quite a bit of alcohol in it and everyone was using it like crazy during those days. I actually once asked about it because I worried the smell from it might be difficult for her to handle while trying to stay sober, but she noted that she could barely smell it even when reaching up to fix her mask, which again goes to show how ridiculous the idea was that someone could smell it on her breath."

"And all of this was shortly before the accident?"

"Yeah."

"But it never came up during the trial?"

"Nope."

"Interesting."

"My guess is the hospital didn't want to be involved. Can you imagine them having to go on record with having failed to detect that she was drinking on the job right before an accident involving kids? That's not a good look at all. And the prosecutor didn't want it on record that the hospital had found no evidence of her drinking, not when the defense already had all these character witnesses that were going to testify on her behalf."

"She did have quite a few it seems," Kelly noted. "Everyone was pretty adamant about how she was not drinking anymore. You, Jill, her AA sponsor."

"And yet the evidence from the accident was clear. There was alcohol in her system."

"Though you initially called that into question," Kelly noted. "Had those tests run to see if her body was somehow converting sugar into alcohol or something."

"Yeah, though I think that is all because I simply didn't want to admit to myself that I had missed the fact that she was still drinking. And honestly, I should have known something wasn't right given that everything had been too easy this time around."

"Too easy?"

"Her getting sober. In the past, it had always been a huge struggle and then she would always backtrack. But this time around, she got sober really fast and stayed sober without issue. No DTs, no late night booze cravings, no drinking mouthwash for a buzz. It was too smooth, too perfect, and yet I believed the lie because I wanted it to be smooth and perfect."

"The lie being that she was staying sober?"

"Yep."

2

"HOW DO YOU TAKE IT?" Don asked a few minutes later while in the kitchen making them coffee.

"Cream and sugar, if you have it," Kelly said.

"You know, you might be in luck ... " Don started, voice fading as he opened the fridge and reached in. "Booya! Beth only drank half of her half-and-half before heading to St. Louis."

"Nice!"

Don brought the carton over to the table, along with the sugar bowl and two mugs, and then went back to waiting on the coffee to finish brewing.

Kelly poured some half-and-half into one of the mugs and then grimaced.

"What?" Don asked.

"The half-and-half. It's totally curdled."

"Seriously?"

"Yep. Though ... " she looked at the side of the carton "... doesn't expire for another two weeks."

"Would it curdle from just sitting in the fridge untouched for a week?" Don asked.

"I wouldn't think so," Kelly said. "Though I use mine every day until it's gone, so ..." she shrugged.

"Well shit, sorry about that."

"It's okay, I'll just drink it black. Like a psychopath."

He chuckled.

"Wow, you can actually smell it now too," she said. "Though ... "

"What?" Don asked.

Kelly leaned in and sniffed her mug and then sniffed at the carton. "Huh."

"What?" he asked again.

"Smell this," she said.

"Ugh, no way!"

"Seriously, just a small sniff."

Don walked over and gave it a sniff.

"What do you think?"

"Huh. Smells like ... I don't know."

"Alcohol," Kelly said.

"Yes!" Then, frowning, "Does half-and-half turn to alcohol if it sits too long?"

"No. Well, anything can turn into alcohol if certain steps are taken, but after just a week in the fridge ... no, not a chance."

"Okay, good."

"Good?"

"I was just thinking, what if that was why Beth had alcohol in her system before the accident all those years ago? What if her half-and-half had turned into alcohol without her knowing it?"

"Yeah, no, if it could happen that easily, morning rush-hours would be like playing Russian roulette."

Don nodded.

"Plus, there were all those vodka bottles in her closet."

"True."

Silence arrived, lasting nearly a minute.

"Are there any in there now?" Kelly asked.

"Any what?"

"Vodka bottles."

"I have no idea."

"Go check."

He did. No vodka bottles.

"Do you think Beth put alcohol in it herself, and then tossed the empties before leaving?" Kelly asked.

"Anything's possible. I mean, she says she's not drinking, but we've clearly been down that road before, though why she would even bother to hide it this time around is beyond me."

"No, no, I mean, do you think she put it in there

before leaving for St. Louis in hopes that you would have some coffee, get pulled over on your way to the office, and then get a DUI?"

"You know, normally I would not discount the possibility of her doing something like that except for the fact that she knows I never put anything in my coffee."

"Oh yeah, good point."

"Plus, I totally would have known there was alcohol in there given the smell."

"Maybe not. I only smelled it after it sat for a bit. If it hadn't looked curdled, and if the coffee had been ready, I would have poured coffee right into it, and the carton would have gone right back into the fridge."

"But you would have tasted it in the coffee once you took a sip. And so would I."

"I'm not sure. With everything all mixed together, I might not have."

"Which leads right back to me always drinking it black, which she knows, so why would she even try to ... oh fuck."

"What?"

"You know how Beth thinks we're totally sleeping together?"

"Yeah."

"What if she put the alcohol in the half-and-half before leaving hoping you might have some the morning after we were together, and then get hit with a DUI or something?"

Kelly contemplated that and then said, "I'll tell you what. If we could somehow prove that she tried something like that, it would be the final nail in her coffin with this custody stuff."

"It could actually go criminal too, couldn't it?"

"It could, but ... I doubt a DA would be interested in such a thing unless an accident had actually happened."

"Hmm."

"I mean, if this was a bar and she was caught tampering with my drink, then yeah, she would be in some serious trouble, but here in a domestic setting, it would be much tougher to nail down any intent given that it is her half-and-half, and she is the only one in the household that drinks it."

He nodded.

"It could even be flipped around if brought up."

"What do you mean?"

"She could try to claim that you or someone with access tampered with the half-and-half knowing that she is the only one who adds it to her coffee, thus hoping she would get another DUI and end up back in jail."

"Oh shit."

"I can picture it now. Her lawyer getting you up on the stand and asking all sorts of questions about who has access to the house, planting all sorts of misdirection seeds into the judge's mind."

"Ugh, that could get really messy."

"Yeah."

A few seconds came and went.

"Now that I'm thinking about it, who has access to the house?" she asked.

"Why?"

"Just curious. I want to be well ahead of this thing if something does spark up."

"Just me, Beth, and the housekeeper."

"What about her friend Jill?"

"You think Jill spiked it?"

"I have no idea, but I do know we caused

some drama in her life with that social media stuff, and if they both think we're sleeping together, maybe she came in one day and spiked it in hopes of getting me in trouble after we got her in trouble."

"That wasn't us, though."

"Yeah, you and I know that, but from her perspective, it's totally us."

Don considered this.

"So, does she?"

"Does she what?"

"Have a key to your house."

"Oh, I don't know, maybe?"

"So you, Beth, the housekeeper, and maybe Jill."

"Yep."

"Anyone else?"

"My mother."

"Your mother has a key?"

"Of course, it's her house."

"No it's not."

"Well, okay, not technically, but she gave us the money for the down payment, so ... "

"Her name's not on it though. It's just you and Beth."

He chuckled.

"What?"

"You sound just like Beth. She used to bring this up all the time. She hated that my mother had a key and would let herself in whenever she felt like it."

"No call or anything, she would just suddenly show up and let herself in?"

"Yeah."

"And that didn't bother you?"

"Well ... sometimes, but like I said, it's her house, so ..."

3

"YOU SPIKED THE HALF-AND-HALF!" Don shouted.

"What?" Beth questioned, still half asleep, phone no longer near her ear given how loud Don's voice was.

"The half-and-half. You spiked it with vodka before you left!"

"What the fuck are you talking about?" Beth demanded.

"You're so lucky we discovered it before drinking any of it," he said. "If we hadn't, and if she had driven somewhere and gotten pulled over, you would be totally fucked."

"She?" Beth asked. "Ah, so now you finally admit to having your fuck-buddy lawyer friend sleeping over when I'm away. Good to know."

"Jesus Christ," Don said. "She stopped by this morning to go over stuff with the divorce and I made us some coffee."

"On a Saturday morning. Good luck getting anyone to believe that." She clicked END and set the phone back onto the coffee table, only to pick it right back up to check the time, her restless night up in the attic making it feel like she had slept way later than was typical.

10:38 AM.

Shit!

She called the hospital to check in on her

mother; her call being bounced around several times before she learned that there was nothing new.

After that, she called Jill.

"Hey," Jill said.

"Random question," Beth said.

"Okay."

"Did you happen to pay a visit to the house after I left and put a bunch of vodka in the half-and-half creamer?"

"Wait? What?"

Beth explained about the call from Don and his accusation that she had put vodka in the half-and-half before leaving in hopes that Kelly would drink some one morning after a night of fucking.

"That's the most ridiculous thing I've ever heard," Jill said.

"Yeah, and yet he was pretty adamant that I spiked the half-and-half before leaving."

"Which you obviously didn't do."

"Nope. And it sounds like you didn't do it either."

"Could he be messing with you, making shit up just to fuck with your mind?"

"I don't think so."

"And he just discovered this now? After you've been gone a week."

"Well, he doesn't put anything in his coffee."

"Oh, right, the lactose intolerance nonsense."

"Yeah, and that's why he thinks this is me attacking Kelly. Like I knew she would be staying the night while I was away and having coffee the next morning."

"Did you even know she puts half-and-half in her coffee?"

"No, and if I did, and if I was going to fuck with her, I'd have put a laxative or something in there. Not vodka."

"Oh my god, that's even better than stink bombing the office. Especially if she had court that day. Can you imagine that, her being all decked out in one of her ruthless power suits, ready to try to eviscerate you on the stand and then, boom, she is running to the bathroom with shit oozing down her stockings."

"I would pay good money to see that happen," Beth said.

"Me too."

"Of course, they would probably somehow figure out it was me and then boom, I'd probably end up back in jail for poisoning her or something."

"You know, maybe that's what this is," Jill said.

"I just told you I didn't spike it," Beth snapped.

"No, jeez, I mean, them trying to make it look like you are trying to harm her by claiming you spiked it."

"Oh. I don't know, seems like overkill since they are totally going to win this thing anyway."

"Yeah."

A few seconds of silence came and went.

"You don't think Don was caught and now is trying to make it look like you were the one spiking it to cover the fact that he was spiking it."

"I don't follow?"

"Like what if he has been spiking your half-and-half with vodka so that you were getting a dose of alcohol every morning, only he forgot to toss out that carton of half-and-half before Kelly was there and she discovered it was spiked? So now he is all like *'Beth must have spiked it hoping you would drink some'* to Kelly to cover himself so that she doesn't start wondering if her client and fuck-buddy was totally trying to get his soon-to-be-ex-wife another DUI."

"What about the fact that I no longer drive?" she asked, her mind suddenly picturing herself getting in her mother's old car and heading up to Chicago.

"Maybe it wasn't to get you another DUI then, but just to make it so you would eventually fall off the wagon and go on a huge bender during the divorce stuff."

Beth contemplated that.

"And didn't you say you felt totally out of sorts the other day, the morning after you arrived at your mother's house?" Jill added.

"I did, but that was after a really long fucked up day."

"Which might have been why you didn't realize you were totally jonesing for a drink."

"I don't know. I think I totally would have tasted it."

"Not with the way you make your coffee. Buckets of cream, ten spoonfuls of sugar. It's like liquid candy by the time you're sipping it."

"No it's not."

"Okay, maybe not liquid candy, but you do put a lot of cream and sugar in there, and you smoke like a chimney which kills your tastebuds. And that coffee that Don makes is so bitter, even I might not notice a slug of vodka in there. Jesus, what if that is why he always makes it so bitter? So you wouldn't notice. I mean, seriously, he puts like seven heaping scoops of grounds in there when four is plenty."

"That's true."

"And then he refused to drive you down here after your mother's accident on the stairs."

"So?"

"So. What if he was hoping you would say fuck it and drive yourself after drinking some of your vodka-laced coffee and get into another — *oh my god!*"

"What?"

"*Your accident.* What if ... " her voice faded, not needing to finish the implication.

4

KELLY GOT CARDED while buying two bottles of vodka and three cartons of half-and-half, the manager that was called over to ring up the purchase waving her on once he saw the nineteen in the birthdate year on her ID.

Purchase secured, she headed back to her apartment and called Liz.

5

BETH WAS LOGGED into the joint bank accounts she still shared with Don, her thumb scrolling through the various purchases he had made in the last several weeks, trying to see if he had bought any hard liquors that he might have been adding to her half-and-half, when a call came in from the hospital.

Her mother had died.

. . .

6

"I DON'T UNDERSTAND," Liz said while looking at the three mugs of coffee that Kelly had set before her. "You just want me to taste them?"

"Yep," Kelly said.

"Why?" Liz asked, suspicion present.

"I can't tell you just yet, but it's important."

Liz's hesitation continued. "And this is really for a case?"

Kelly nodded.

"I don't remember any of our cases involving coffee, but whatever," she said and reached for the first mug to take a sip, her eyes staring at Kelly the entire time.

A sip from the second mug and then the third mug followed, Liz giving a bit of a frown after the third one, which was interesting because that was the only one that didn't have any vodka in it.

"Can you tell me what is different about each one?" Kelly asked.

"I think ... " Liz started, but then stopped, her hand reaching for the first mug again and taking a sip. She then took another sip from each of the other two as well. "Do they each have the same amount of sugar?"

"Yep," Kelly confirmed.

"And same kind of coffee?"

"Good old Folgers. Medium roast."

"Ugh. You really need to start using good beans and a French press."

"Yeah, yeah, quit stalling," Kelly said. "Or

admit you can't tell what the difference is between each one."

Liz picked up the second mug and took a sip, and then did the same with the third, licking her lips afterward. Not as a sign of enjoyment, but of contemplation.

"Different creamers. First two are legit dairy ones, though one has less fat than the other I think. The third is some sort of alternative soy or almond or some other non-dairy crap."

"Each one has the same full-bodied half-and-half."

"Really?"

"Yep."

Liz frowned.

"In fact, each one has the exact same coffee, half-and-half creamer, and sugar in it, and yes, the sugar in each is real sugar."

"Okay then, something to do with the mugs? These two are fancy porcelain and this one is ... something really cheap from Target?"

Kelly laughed at that. "They're all from Target."

"I give up then."

"This one" — she pointed to the third mug — "is the only one that doesn't have any vodka in it."

7

"YOU NEED to make a decision by tomorrow," his mother said.

"I can't," Don said after taking a deep breath.

"We'll do the Heritage Academy then," his

mother said. "It doesn't have the highest ratings, but I've been assured from various sources that the young ladies from that school are all of a higher caliber than what is being allowed into the other — "

"No, I mean I can't send her away," he said.

"Donald, you can't raise a child on your own while advancing yourself the way we have planned, and the chances of finding a woman of good standing to care for her while you are away from home is nearly impossible these days given that the industry has been taken over by women who have crossed the — "

"Mom, stop," he said, voice a bit forceful. "I've decided I'm not sending her away, nor am I hiring someone to be a mother for her."

"I see. You're in one of your little moods today."

"I'm not in any mood," he said. "I just don't want to send my daughter away. She belongs here with me and her mother."

"We'll talk tomorrow when you're more clearheaded."

"Mom — " he started, only to realize she had disconnected the call.

He sighed and set the phone down, his eyes going back to the wedding album he had pulled down from the shelf. Page after page of Beth smiling while looking beautiful in a gown that his mother and her friends had all called the 'white lie' given that she was pregnant during the wedding itself. One of them had even shouted "remember that she is eating for two" while Don was cutting a piece of cake for Beth, which had caused Beth's lips to tremble a bit as they stood beneath the spotlight. Tears had been present later while they did their first dance, tears that some had thought were due to happiness, but which he knew were not.

She was happy. There was no doubt about that. He was too. But there were times when that was not enough of a shield to stop the constant bombardment from those on his side of the family who had clearly been determined to humiliate her every chance they got.

8

"SO THIS IS INTERESTING," Liz said, twisting her I-pad so that Kelly could see it, the table beyond sporting a frat-house like display of vodka bottles, half-and-half cartons, and coffee mugs, the two having gone about testing how much vodka could be added to a carton of half-and-half before it just became too much for even the most tastebud-challenged person to notice.

Kelly examined the screen, but couldn't figure out what it was that Liz was directing her toward, her mind a bit buzzed from all the taste tests she had done herself. "What?"

"Caffeine and its impact on alcohol," Liz said, seemingly unfazed by her own booze consumption, which had gone far beyond the initial three mugs. "According to this, which may not be official at all given that anything can look impressive online, caffeine nullifies the depressive aspects of booze while the stimulants in the caffeine continue to work their magic, making it so the alcohol can be more potent than when consumed on its own because a person doesn't feel the negative effects of the alcohol and typically drinks more of it."

"Meaning that it is possible Beth, or anyone who was unknowingly drinking vodka-laced coffee, wouldn't even know they were drinking alcohol because they weren't really feeling the negative effects right away."

"Exactly."

Kelly didn't reply to that.

"You know, even if it's all complete nonsense, the what if possibility it presents is very troubling," Liz said.

"It really is," Kelly agreed.

"Are you going to mention any of this to Don?"

"I don't know."

"If you do, it will get back to his mother, and then you will be out of a job. As will I. And given all her contacts and political clout ... well ... I don't have to tell you how fucked we would be."

Kelly nodded.

Liz sipped some water and said, "You want to know what the crazy thing about this is?"

"What?"

"I'm convinced she is capable of this. Like, totally convinced. No doubts whatsoever."

"Me too."

"Kind of tells you what a cold-hearted bitch she is."

"I know, right?"

"And now I'm totally bummed out about it because if his mother did do this, and if Beth was unknowingly drinking a bit of vodka every day with her coffee before that accident, it means she totally got away with it, and will continue to get away with it."

"Unless ... "

"What? Go all Tom Cruise *'you can't handle the truth!'* on her and get her to admit what she did?" Liz shook her head. "Would never happen. Not on this side of a movie screen. His mother is way too smooth."

9

BETH'S AFTERNOON was a complete blur, her movements almost trance-like as she went from office to office at the hospital to speak with various officials, one of whom was somewhat insistent that she sign a waiver forgoing autopsy.

She knew better than that, her time spent working in hospitals having taught her that if the hospital didn't want an autopsy, it was because they feared a malpractice lawsuit following the documented discoveries made during the autopsy.

MRSA was her guess.

Hospitals were breeding grounds for such infections, and if one was revealed during an autopsy, she would barely have to lift a finger before the hospital lawyers offered a settlement so that things wouldn't go to trial and create publicity.

A text from Jill was waiting for her that evening when she arrived home with Belle, one that was asking if she had found any evidence of Don having purchased booze that he could have been adding to her half-and-half.

Nope, Beth said to herself, a decision to hold off on telling Jill about her mother's death arriving given that she would drop everything and come down.

Nothing but restaurant and gas station purchases had been in Don's purchase history during this period, the most recent being from the night before when he had filled up his car at the BP gas station near the house.

A full tank of gas.

She bolted up from the chair, an idea forming.

A few seconds later she was in the garage, staring at a coiled up hose, one which she quickly clipped down to a more manageable size with a set of hedge clippers and tossed into the trunk of her mother's car.

10

AFTER GOING through the wedding album picture by picture, Don found himself pulling out other various albums from the shelves that featured the early days of his relationship with Beth, several of which actually pre-dated the wedding itself since they had been together for nearly five years before he finally took the step and proposed to her.

Pictures of that proposal had been captured by Jill who had known exactly when and where it would take place. She had actually helped him pick out the ring as well, Don having called her in a panic from the jewelry store, completely overwhelmed by the rings available and unable to figure out which one would be perfect for Beth.

A magical moment, one that he would give anything to go back and experience again. And then again, and again, and again, as well as all the other happy moments the two had shared together.

Sadly, such was not possible.

Unless ...

A vision of himself down on one knee again appeared before his eyes, only he wasn't reliving the past experience but creating a new one, complete with a new ring and proposal, this one being one of reunification and a promise that they would put to rest the ugliness of the last few years and move forward with a fresh start.

Was such a thing really possible?

Could they actually mend things?

He wished he could call Jill to ask about this, but that bridge had been completely burned. Any calls he made to her would go unanswered, and if by chance they were answered, he doubted she would hear what he had to say even if she did allow him a moment to speak.

No.

The only person he could really speak with about these things was Kelly.

11

"ICE CREAM!" Belle shouted, while giving a little hop and a clap of her hands.

Beth smiled, and then said, "Okay, you go wait in the family room while I open everything in the kitchen and make sure it isn't all melty from them driving it over."

"Okay!" Belle zoomed away, her tiny pajama-clad body disappearing through a wall cutout on the right, all while Beth continued toward the kitchen doorway at the end of the hallway.

Two minutes later, she was handing over the giant ice cream treat to Belle who quickly dug into it with a zeal that only kids could display, a zeal that Beth knew would be systematically crushed once she was sent to one of the boarding schools Don and his mother would be sending her too.

12

IT DIDN'T TAKE LONG for the crushed up sleeping pills to take effect, Belle drifting away before she even finished the ice cream, Beth carrying her up into the bedroom and tucking her into the sheets before heading out to the garage, a bag of energy drinks in hand.

13

DON WAS A MESS.

Kelly realized this fairly quickly after answering the phone and hearing the emotion in his voice, her role in this conversation one of simply being an ear as he talked about all the good times he and Beth had shared together, and the possibility that they could put all the ridiculous drama behind them in an attempt to start fresh.

Silence arrived about twenty minutes in.

Kelly waited.

"I just don't know what to do," Don finally said.

"No one ever does in these situations, which is what makes everything so difficult."

Several more seconds of silence followed.

"Have you spoken to her at all recently?" Kelly asked.

"No, not really."

Several more seconds of silence.

"Do you think I should?" he asked.

"As your lawyer, I'd say no. One-on-one conversations without any legal counsel present are never a good idea once things reach this stage. As your friend, I would say that you should really think things over, and if after a day or two you still are feeling like you might want to give things another chance, then we can figure out a way of feeling her out and seeing what her thoughts on this are, and whether it truly is something that could unfold."

Don didn't reply to this.

"One thing I would strongly advise against is making any kind of outreach toward her while in the state you are in right now," she added.

"Yeah, you're probably right," he said.

Nothing else followed. Kelly eventually ending the call by suggesting he get some sleep and then tomorrow they could get together for some coffee and talk about things again.

14

"WHOA, WHOA, BELLE, SLOW DOWN," Robert Flynn said, eyes blinking away the sleep that had just barely gotten started before his phone began to ring. He looked at his watch. 11:15 PM. "What do you mean you can't find your mom?"

15

A FEW MINUTES LATER, Belle was opening the door for him after glancing at him through the side window, the look of fright that was on her face causing him to crouch down and open his arms for her.

Tear-laced statements about waking up with a tummy-ache and throwing up and then hearing the monster who wouldn't be quiet and then trying to find her mommy echoed from her lips, all while he held her, his hands rubbing her back, soothing words leaving his lips, the moment bringing back memories of another time he had stood in this same doorway offering words of comfort while someone sobbed into his shoulder.

Only this time it was a nine-year-old girl in pajamas rather than a young wife and mother who had just found her husband hanging in the attic amid the pieces of a smashed easel and several slashed paintings.

16

DON OPENED HIS EYES, a sound having yanked him from an odd dream with a courtroom setting, one where Kelly, Liz, Jill, and Beth were all badgering him as he sat on the witness stand while his mother was the judge watching over everything, gavel in hand.

Someone was in the bedroom with him, their body barely visible in the glow from the bathroom light that he always left on.

"Kelly?" he asked, pushing himself up onto his elbows.

A shriek echoed, followed by something crashing into his head.

Darkness arrived.

17

BETH STARED in horror as Don began to spasm on the bed, his arms and legs flopping all over the place while blood oozed from the top of his head.

She looked down at the snow globe she held, one that had been an odd wedding gift to them from Jill, spots of blood now staining the glass while the snow within swirled around the tiny bride and groom that stood inside.

Using it as a weapon had not been on her mind when picking it up. Instead, she had simply caught sight of it in the glow from the bathroom light, an unexpected longing for the happiness she and Don had once shared arriving without warning.

Thunk.

She looked up.

Don had fallen to the floor, his body having spasmed itself right off of the bed.

Uncertainty arrived, as did pity.

She hit him a second time.

And then a third time.

And a fourth.

And a fifth.

Over and over again, her mind losing count after the sixth or seventh hit, her goal simply being to make him stop twitching, the blows finally coming to a halt when his skull had a fist-sized hole in it.

She dropped the snow globe, the glass portion finally shattering as it met the floor.

Blood.

It was everywhere.

Piss too, and a horrible fecal smell.

She would never be able to clean all this up, not in a way that would hide the fact that Don had been attacked and likely killed while sleeping, her initial idea of making it look like he had simply vanished into thin air no longer something she could pull off.

EIGHT

I

BELLE WAS sound asleep as Beth looked in upon her early the next morning, the crushed up sleeping pills having apparently worked like a charm.

Beth yawned, the sight of her daughter snuggled up beneath the sheets acting like a siren call toward her own desires for sleep, her body wanting nothing more than to curl up in the blankets on the couch.

First things first though she needed to wash the last of the Monster and gasoline taste from her mouth, her first-ever experience with siphoning gasoline from a vehicle five hours earlier resulting in a mouthful of fuel that she couldn't help but spew out all over the floor of the garage while struggling to get the end of the hose into the gas tank of her mother's car.

Following that, she had repeatedly gargled and spit mouthfuls of Monster, the flavor of the potent energy drink doing little to remove the wretched taste of the gasoline from her mouth.

The fact that some of the fuel had spilled down the front of her shirt didn't help, the normally enjoyable scent doing nothing but acting as a reminder of the disgusting experience.

It wasn't until she was driving through Bloomington when the nearly overwhelming taste, and the vomit-tickle in the back of her throat, finally began to yield to the Monsters she was chugging, though it never fully faded.

A bottle of Tabasco sauce was in the fridge.

Putting it to her lips, Beth tossed back several swigs of it as if it were a mini-bottle of booze.

Ugh!

Swishing Tabasco sauce was not pleasant at all, but it seemed to do the trick.

A yawn arrived.

She needed to lie down before her body decided the kitchen floor was suitable enough, the caffeine from the energy drinks no longer able to fuel her consciousness.

Stumbling into the family room, she started shuffling herself over to the couch, her body halfway there when she froze, a tiny gasp escaping her lips.

Mr. Flynn was sound asleep in a chair.

2

KELLY TOSSED and turned most of the night, her mind unable to stop thinking about the possibility that Beth's half-and-half had been spiked by Don's mother, which then kept leading to thoughts on what her possible actions could be in regards to this possibility.

Liz had been adamant about there being nothing she could do.

In a movie, her character would heroically confront the perpetrator of such an awful act and get them to admit what it was they had done, but in real life, that just wouldn't fly. Don's mother would never break in such a way.

But what about Don?

Could she convince him that his mother was behind this?

Liz had warned her against attempting such a thing, her thinking being that Don would go right to his mother with her theory, not in an attempt to get Kelly into trouble, but in a confrontational way, which would quickly fade given the hold his mother maintained on him.

But maybe Liz was wrong.

Maybe ...

3

"... he'll finally snip the umbilical cord?" Liz asked. "Not a chance. No way, no how."

"I don't know," Kelly said. "I think he is so close. I mean, he clearly still loves Beth. That's been obvious since day one. And you and I both know he has always had serious reservations about going through with the divorce."

"Yes, he does, but even so, he is still going through with it, which just goes to show that when push comes to shove, his mother will always have her way with him."

"Hmm."

"Hmm," Liz mirrored.

"Ugh, I hate it when you do that," Kelly noted.

"That's because you know that I know that you do that when you know I'm right, but can't quite admit it yet."

"Hmm."

Liz chuckled and then let out a sudden curse.

"What happened?" Kelly asked.

"Nothing. I'm making breakfast for Lacy and got popped by bacon grease."

"Ouch."

"And right on my tit!"

"What? Is Lacy having you cook bacon naked again?"

"No, I have a collar and heels on, plus a leather harness that is holding a giant vibrating — oh Jesus butt fuck!"

Kelly pulled the phone away from her face as she let out a snort, and then said, "I better let you go so you can focus. No telling what will happen if you ruin her breakfast."

"If it doesn't ruin me first," Liz said and then gasped a third time. A string of cuss words followed.

Kelly stared at the phone for a moment after disconnecting the call, once again amazed by the bizarre relationship Liz and Lacy shared, and then went to refill her coffee. That in hand, she headed into the family room where she had a notepad open on the coffee table, a list of things that she would need to do in order to start up her own legal practice being made.

· · ·

4

MOMMY.

She heard the voice through a fog but couldn't really make sense of it, not until her body was being shaken while the voice echoed the word over and over again.

"Mommy!"

Beth opened her eyes, confusion dominating.

She felt awful.

And sick.

A moment later, she was nearly knocking Belle out of the way as she ran to the bathroom, the vomit that came up tasting unlike anything she had ever experienced before. And she had spent many a morning with her head in the toilet bowl, so she certainly was an expert in such tastes.

"Mommy, are you okay?" Belle asked when she came back, a look of concern spread across her tiny face.

"No, no, I'm fine. Just something I drank last night."

"No!"

This caught her off guard. "Oh, sweetheart, I didn't mean that kind of drinking. It was something else. Like with the milk the other day. You know I don't ever drink alcohol anymore."

"Does this mean daddy won't be sad now?"

"Daddy was sad?"

"When you were away. He always pretended it was just allergies like people do on TV, but I knew he was sad and missed you."

Beth didn't know how to reply to this.

Blood.

Brain tissue.

Kelly.

He had said her name.

At night.

While in bed.

When her name would have no business echoing from his lips.

And after she had been there that morning drinking coffee.

Drinking my half-and-half.

Which apparently had been spiked.

Only why would they have just then learned about it?

This last thought halted all other thoughts.

If her half-and-half had been spiked with alcohol as Don had stated, and if those two were fucking each other every night like she envisioned, then Kelly would have noticed the half-and-half being spiked long before yesterday.

Unless they normally stayed at her place?

"Mommy? Do you?"

"Do I what?" she asked, eyes blinking a few times.

"Do you want me to call Mr. Flynn to bring you some 7-Up?"

"No, no, I'm" — she stopped for a second and then asked, "Call Mr. Flynn? You know his number?"

"Yes," she said, nodding. "It's on a sticky note by the phone. He put it there in case we ever needed his help with anything."

Beth went to the phone, which hung on the wall in the kitchen, her eyes having never really looked at it given that she used her cell phone for everything.

Sure enough, a green sticky note was right next to it with Mr. Flynn's number on it, one that he had clearly put there for Belle since he had watched as Beth put the number in her phone the first time he had babysat for her.

He was worried about me and wanted Belle to have this should I ever go crazy.

Only what did he think he could do if I ever did go crazy?

Not like he could rush over here and overpower me.

Last night had pretty much proved that.

It clicked.

"Honey, did you call Mr. Flynn last night?"

Belle looked down at the kitchen floor, almost as if she could sense something in Beth's tone that told her she did not want to answer truthfully with this one.

"Why did you call him?" Beth asked.

"I was scared and couldn't find you," she said, lips starting to quiver.

"Oh sweetie, it's okay," she said, hugging Belle.

Belle started sobbing.

"You must not have realized I was sleeping in grandma's room last night."

"You were?" Belle asked, confusion appearing as she wiped her nose.

"Uh-huh, the couch hurts my back."

Belle frowned. "But I didn't see you in there?"

"That's because it is a huge bed with all those giant pillows, so I look pretty small. But now you know, so if anyone ever asks if I was here last night, you can tell them I was in grandma's bed, okay?"

Belle nodded.

"And you know what?" Beth said, still a bit unsettled. "I have a surprise for you."

"You do?" Belle asked, a glow appearing upon her cheeks.

"I do. I was going to wait a few days, but I think today is better than waiting."

"What is it?"

"We actually have to go out and get it, so why don't you go change out of your pajamas while I go get us an Uber?"

5

TWO MISSED CALLS.

Both were from Don, one of which didn't surprise her since she had made the call herself from his phone up in Chicago, his cooling thumb used to unlock the device, her hope being that a call from him up there while her phone was left down here in St. Louis would help add weight to the alibi she would give on her being in St. Louis herself at the time of his murder and thus not the one responsible.

The other call had actually been from him earlier in the evening while still alive, likely around the time that she would have been near Lincoln, Illinois.

Whatever his reason for calling her was unknown since he hadn't left a message.

They will ask me about these and why I didn't answer.

Actually, they would probably be asking her all kinds of questions, and while they would go about it in a casual way, the questioning itself would be an attempt to trip her up and reveal to them how she did it since she would be their prime suspect. The spouse always was. And while they would note she had been in St. Louis at the time of the murder — if her phone call from his phone to her phone worked as intended — they would do everything they could to try to figure out if she had hired someone to do the deed for her.

Fortunately, any look they made into her time spent in jail would reveal nothing but the frequency of the abuse she had suffered at the hands of her fellow inmates, all of which had been well documented by how often she had been a guest of the infirmary.

"Mommy, I'm ready!" Belle called.

"Okay," Beth replied and quickly opened the Uber app so she could book them a ride to the local pet store.

6

KELLY WAS SURPRISED when she saw the name displayed on her Caller ID, her initial thought being that Don's mother had somehow found out about her theory into her having been spiking Beth's half-and-half with vodka. In reality, the woman was simply concerned because Don had not shown up to church that morning.

"Nope," Kelly said. "I haven't seen or heard from him at all today."

"I see."

"Want me to go check to see if he's okay?"

"Would you?"

"Yep."

7

THE CRIES from the cat carrier were heartbreaking, but Beth knew they were just temporary and that once the two kittens were inside the house and free from the carrier, the frightened cries would be replaced with curiosity as they explored their new surroundings.

A police officer was on the front porch as they pulled up to the house.

Already? Beth said to herself, somewhat startled.

But then she noticed a Missouri patch on the sleeve of the officer's uniform, which meant this likely had nothing to do with Don.

Not yet.

Instead ...

She looked up the street and saw a patrol car parked on the corner in front of Mr. Flynn's house, another officer heading the opposite way down the sidewalk.

This was also quicker than she had anticipated.

"Afternoon," Beth said to the officer after instructing Belle to head into the kitchen with the carrier, but not to open it yet.

"Afternoon," the officer replied, and then proceeded to explain that they were simply asking everyone in the neighborhood if they had seen a Mr. Robert Flynn, the elderly gentleman who lived on the corner.

"No, I haven't," Beth said, the lie slipping from

her lips with ease. "My daughter and I have actually been out all morning picking out kittens. Her grandmother died yesterday, so I figure this might help ease her grief."

"Aww, I'm so sorry to hear that," the officer said.

"Thank you," Beth replied.

An awkward silence arrived.

"Is there a number I should call if I happen to see him?"

"Oh um, yes, just the local precinct," he said, clearly uncomfortable and wanting to move on. "We're hoping to find him quickly since his family says he has a fairly serious heart condition that requires daily medication."

Heart condition.

Daily medication.

Oh fuck.

"Anyway, sorry to hear about the grandmother," he added. "Hope the kittens help."

Beth nodded a thanks and then, once the officer was beyond the porch, hurried inside, her panic rising as she made her way toward Belle's bedroom.

Belle was standing in the middle of the room, staring at the wall.

Beth stared at it as well.

"Mommy, why is my wall beeping?"

Milton Keynes UK
Ingram Content Group UK Ltd.
UKHW040946071123
432124UK00001B/2

9 781734 876338